Text copyright © 2013 by Ammi-Joan Paquette
Jacket art copyright © 2013 by Steve Stone

All rights reserved. Published in the United States by Random House Children's Books, a division of Random House, Inc., New York.

Random House and the colophon are registered trademarks of Random House, Inc.

Visit us on the Web! randomhouse.com/teens

Educators and librarians, for a variety of teaching tools, visit us at
RHTeachersLibrarians.com

Library of Congress Cataloging-in-Publication Data
Paquette, Ammi-Joan.
Paradox / A.J. Paquette. — 1st ed.
p. cm.
Summary: When Ana finds herself on a desolate alien planet with no memory of her past, she must survive and discover her mission to save the Earth from a fearsome virus.
ISBN 978-0-375-86962-4 (trade) — ISBN 978-0-375-96962-1 (lib. bdg.)
ISBN 978-0-375-98438-9 (ebook) — ISBN 978-0-375-87163-4 (pbk.)
[1. Science fiction. 2. Interplanetary voyages—Fiction. 3. Survival—Fiction.
4. Amnesia—Fiction. 5. Memory—Fiction. 6. Virus diseases—Fiction.] I. Title.
PZ7.P2119Par 2013   [E]—dc23   2012006431

Printed in the United States of America

10 9 8 7 6 5 4 3 2 1

First Edition

Random House Children's Books supports
the First Amendment and celebrates the right to read.

PARADOX

Text copyright © 2013 by Ammi-Joan Paquette
Jacket art copyright © 2013 by Steve Stone

Visit us on the Web! randomhouse.com/teens

Educators and librarians, for a variety of teaching tools, visit us at RHTeachersLibrarians.com

Library of Congress Cataloging-in-Publication Data
Paquette, Ammi-Joan.
Paradox / A.J. Paquette. — 1st ed.
p. cm.
Summary: When Ana finds herself on a desolate alien planet with no memory of her past, she must survive and discover her mission to save the Earth from a fearsome virus.
ISBN 978-0-375-86962-4 (trade) — ISBN 978-0-375-96962-1 (lib. bdg.)
ISBN 978-0-375-98438-9 (ebook) — ISBN 978-0-375-87163-4 (pbk.)
[1. Science fiction. 2. Interplanetary voyages—Fiction. 3. Survival—Fiction.
4. Amnesia—Fiction. 5. Memory—Fiction. 6. Virus diseases—Fiction.] I. Title.
PZ7.P2119Par 2013   [E]—dc23   2012006431

Printed in the United States of America

10 9 8 7 6 5 4 3 2 1

First Edition

for Kim, who was there with Ana from the start

Part 1

Newly Discovered Planet Confirmed to Be Habitable

Global News Syndicate

The International Astronomical Union confirmed Friday that newly discovered exoplanet Cyclid-Bf is almost certainly habitable. First detected last month within the twin star system of Cyclid, the planet has only one third the mass of Earth, yet shows signs of deeply buried groundwater and a surface temperature capable of supporting plant life.

The planet's distance from Earth—nearly 35 light-years—is minuscule by galactic standards. However, even employing the most cutting-edge technology, a manned space mission would take many thousands of years to arrive. "Cyclid-Bf appears to be in every way ideal for supporting human life," said eminent astrophysicist Dr. Alan Bartleby. "Yet any humans actually trying to get there would perish long before arrival. Humanity may have just found its ultimate paradox."

PARADOX

for Kim, who was there with Ana from the start

ONE

`00:27:52:29`

This is how she wakes. There is a heavy pressure on her chest and a dull weight in her legs. Her mouth feels like cotton and the air is stale. Her eyes are glued shut.

No . . . not glued. She thinks they might open, if she tries. She tries.

Her eyes are open now, but she can't see any difference. The room—*is it a room?*—is pitch-black, a solid wall of dark.

Flash!

A pulse of red light explodes in the darkness. She clamps her eyes shut again, but the brightness scours the backs of her lids. She takes quick, shallow breaths as the burst of light fades.

Flash! Another takes its place, then another.

Behind closed lids, her eyes are starting to adjust. She forces them back open. Fiery light-shadows streak around her, shadows that look alive.

Flash!

She shifts her head and looks down, trying to assess her condition in these quick bloody snapshots hemmed in by viscous darkness.

She's strapped to a padded chair with armrests and a propped-up leg support that goes out past her feet. A dark band stretches across her upper thighs; another two crisscross her chest. She arches her body, pushing against the bands, but there's no give. She can feel her skin starting to bruise and she slows her frantic efforts. There has to be a way out of this.

Flash!

The room is as round as a bucket, skinny with a high, dome-shaped ceiling but otherwise empty. She digs her fingers into the strap across her thighs and tries to pry it up. Nothing. With her fingertips she follows the band to the edges of her chair. *Like a seat belt, maybe that's what these are?* But she can find no spring-release button.

Flash!

What's going on?

Flash!

Where am I?

Flash!

The pulses are coming from somewhere to her left. She reaches out in the direction of the light, feeling for the wall.

There! She finds something flat and round. A button. She pushes her palm against it.

The belts around her chest and the wide one on her thighs snap open. There's a sudden sharp pricking below her waist, almost like something pulling out of her skin. She catches the band that was on her lower body and sees a row of long, thin prongs along the underside. On the front of the belt is a row of fine print, one label assigned to each prong: ELIMINATION . . . FLUID . . . LIFE SUPPORT . . .

A violent shudder ripples through her body. *What is going on?*

Letting go of the belt, she bends forward at the waist and stretches her ankles and knees, groaning as her muscles shift position for the first time in what feels like quite a while.

A second later, the red light on the wall goes off and a flashing green one takes its place. She turns her head to the left and sees that the green light is coming from a second button, right next to the first.

Is this some kind of a game? Her heart beats faster as she presses the new button.

Bright white light floods the room. She throws her hands over her eyes, but the light pushes through her fingers and cuts into her. Too bright. Too white.

And that's when she notices.

Her mind is white, too. Blank.

It's strange, because she can picture and name all the objects in her little room—the chair, the walls, the seat belts. She stretches her mind and thinks of cars, computers, pepperoni pizza, ice-cold root beer. But all these objects float like ghosts in her mind. There's no one in the car. The root beer has no flavor. The computer is static, its screen dark. She knows *about* all these things, but she doesn't *know* them. They are not attached to any memories.

What about her? Where does *she* come from?

She blinks under her hands.

Who am I?

With a shock she realizes that she has no idea. Here's what she knows about her world: A tall, round room. Bands across her thighs and over her chest. A red light that pulses and a green light that is pressed, and then a white so bright it cuts through everything else.

That's it—her history, her memory, her now.

This is the first chapter of her life.

Panic rises up inside her, squeezing like a fist. She stays sitting for what seems like a long time, hands still shielding her eyes from that too-white light, while somewhere nearby a very low sound goes *tick, tick, tick*. Gradually, the quiet rubs away at her fear until the sharp edge dulls and her heart rate begins to slow.

Sliding her hands off her face, blinking a little as her eyes adjust, she looks down at her body. She doesn't recognize it, not the lanky arms or the long legs or the lumpy vest over a gray jumpsuit that covers her from neck to ankle. The heavy-duty black boots. The little white square that's pinned to her chest.

Wait. The *what?*

The nametag! She is wearing a nametag.

It's small, an ordinary slip of paper inside a flimsy plastic label, held in place on her jumpsuit with a silver pin. She tugs the pin free with trembling fingers.

Yes. The paper has a word on it, three printed black letters in the upper right corner: ANA. That's the only thing on the tag—the rest is completely blank. But it's enough to start.

Ana. The name is a wave that lifts her and a hand that holds her and a boat that carries her away. It's a compass that says: Head this way! It's a banner that tells her: All is not lost.

She recognizes it immediately. It's her own name.

Feeling somehow stronger with this knowledge inside her, Ana sets the nametag down on the armrest of her chair and turns her attention to the tiny room. The walls are checkered like a quilt, each square padded with velvety red cushion and edged in polished gray metal. The ceiling, studded with fluorescent lightbulbs, rises to a narrow peak high above her, and is also lined with puffy cushioning.

She doesn't see the belts that had been holding her. Did they retract into her seat? She looks down over the side. The chair sits on a pole—*like a dentist's chair . . . but have I ever gone to the dentist?*—and underneath is a yawning black space. A grille walkway surrounds her seat and bridges the gap between her chair and the far wall, where there's a door set into the red padding. *A door!* It's an odd oblong shape, like some kind of a portal or a hatch, and made of solid-looking metal.

Ana slides off the seat and plants her feet on the walkway, her legs shaking a little at first. As she stands all the way up, her hand brushes something on her right hip: a tough nylon sheath with a smooth, dark handle at the top. Instinctively, she reaches across her body with her left hand, grasps the handle, and pulls it free to reveal a twelve-inch dagger made of a matte, nonreflective metal and with an edge so sharp it looks like it could cut steel.

What? Heart hammering, Ana slides the blade back into place. She glances down at the bulky vest she's wearing—bulky because it hides more weapons?

Ana looks back at the door. She has no idea where it leads, but it's suddenly clear that there will be no lighthearted surprise party waiting for her on the other side.

Still a little unsteady on her feet, she crosses the grille walkway to the door. A bar-shaped handle bisects it at hip level; to one side of the door is a small, dark screen. *A fingerpad.* Without thinking, Ana presses her index finger against the screen.

Her stomach is churning. *Making fear soup,* she thinks, and the thought makes her smile. In spite of all the uncertainty surrounding her, Ana's heart lifts. Her mind might be broken, but that expression had to come from somewhere, didn't it? Maybe there are more fragments of the past drifting around her mind space, bits of her old self waiting to drop in at some random moment, when she least expects it.

The fingerpad beeps, and she hears a series of clicks and

whirrs from inside the door as the locking mechanism begins to disengage. She reaches for the handle.

And that's when she sees it. On the lower half of the door there is a mesh pocket, and sticking out of the pocket is the edge of something that looks like paper.

Ana reaches down and pulls the paper free. It's an envelope with one word written in careful block print, the same word that was on her nametag, her word: *Ana*. Inside the envelope is a sheet of paper.

She slides the sheet out and unfolds it. Her eyes run over the handwritten words.

Ana:

You have now arrived on Paradox. I realize that you must have questions, but I can give you no answers at this time. You will not remember who I am, nor will you recollect the events that have led you to this place.

That is as it should be. You have undergone a procedure known as surgical retrograde amnesia. You have no memory of your past, and you are on unfamiliar ground, but your body has been well trained. You have been sent to Paradox with a specific mission: Experience. Discover. Survive.

Experience your surroundings; follow the preset path of your journey with a careful eye to anything that might be worthy of observation. Discover what is hidden, looking below the surface for things that might be out of the ordinary. And survive, for if you do not then all of this will be in vain. Your body is its own record. Be mindful of the countdown.

   Your world—our world—is on the brink of disaster. Your mission must succeed. If not, I cannot vouchsafe your future.

                    With regards toward your best success,
                              J. R. Pritchett

Ana stands still for a long time, trying to process all this new information. Paradox? J. R. Pritchett? Surgical retrograde amnesia? None of it makes any sense. They're all just words, ideas with no weight behind them—nothing like her name, which came alive when she saw it.

Looking down at the paper again, she notices something else. Scribbled at the bottom in smudged black ink—written in a shaky hand, different from the main note—are two letters: O+O

What is that supposed to mean?

What does *any* of it mean?

She starts to crumple the letter, then stops and folds it over and over until it's a flat square that can fit in the hollow of her palm. She finds a pocket on the front of her suit and slides it inside. The panic in her gut, the cold emptiness of all she doesn't know, is so strong it's almost numbing. But she has to get moving.

Broken or not, there's only one way she's going to find answers.

The fingerpad flashes green, and Ana grasps the door handle. The bar moves easily under her weight. With a gentle *hisssss*, then a *click*, the door unlatches.

Ana pushes and the door swings open.

She is greeted by an endless swath of dry brown earth. Giant boulders that are gray and black and dull green and even coral pink are scattered across the landscape. She realizes she's looking from a height, and as she pushes the door wider, she sees it's a ten- or twelve-foot drop to the ground. Off ahead a cliff cuts across the horizon, so far away it's barely more than a haze in the distance.

And the sky . . . she tilts her head back. The sky is pink! It's as if she were inside a huge peach, the top half of the world streaked with ribbons of orange and yellow and red—and, yes, cheek-blushing pink. Over it all hangs a watery yellow sun.

What is this place?

The wind hits her then, a gust of chilly-fresh air that takes her breath away for a second, and she leans into it, pushing the door out until it's flat against the outer wall and it latches into place.

That's when she sees it. Over the horizon way off to her left, low over the distant cliff wall, looms a *second* sun.

TWO

00:27:08:13

Two suns? That's not right. And yet, there they are, one dim and high overhead and the other lolling white-hot on the horizon.

Is this a sign that the strings inside her are broken worse than she'd thought? Or is it something else?

Some*where* else?

She should be seeing buildings. She should be seeing trees. There should be signs of roads and cars. Planes, maybe. Instead, there's just dry, empty land, and the wind beating against the heavy door, and *two* suns pulsing in the raspberry sky.

She thinks about the letter and its talk of exploring, of discovering, of trying to save her world, almost as if—*You have now arrived on Paradox*—as if that world that needed saving were somewhere else. Somewhere not here.

No way. That's ridiculous . . . isn't it?

And yet the more she thinks about it, the more the idea fits, sliding into another one of those gaps in her mind with a perfect fit. Gripping the doorframe, Ana steps up onto the threshold, teetering a little as the wind whips across the doorway. She considers the drop and wonders what to do next, but even as she thinks it, her right hand is reaching toward a heavy-duty switch in the doorframe. She flips the switch in a practiced motion, as if she's done it countless times before, and a mechanical *whirr* fills the air. A second later a staircase is unfolding beneath her feet, the base hitting the ground with a resounding *boom*.

Your body has been well trained, the letter told her. She's just starting to understand what that means. She steps onto the top step and finds it surprisingly solid. Well trained or not, her legs are shaking, and for a few moments she focuses on tensing and releasing the muscles until she gets herself under control.

These are running legs, she suddenly knows. She has a flash of a foot hitting a puddle, water arcing out in a brown swell; athletic shoes slapping on concrete; bare toes tamping down soft black rubber. *Thud, thud, thud.* There's no body or face attached to the image, but she senses the movement in those legs and knows they are hers.

It's not a memory, exactly, but it's a piece of her all the same. A ripple of warmth floods her chest.

Carefully, Ana climbs down the staircase. Only when she reaches the ground does she allow herself to turn and look at the place she's left.

Two suns . . . A pink sky . . . She has a definite idea about what she's going to see, but still—a thrill courses through her to observe the tall, conical body, solid and gleaming as it rests on its round, squat bottom, nose pointing to the sky.

She's just climbed out of a rocket ship.

Metallic red, scratched up in places, the rocket reaches four or five times her height. Still, it doesn't seem very big for a ship that has apparently carried her to this alien world. To this . . .

She forms the word in her mind, then says it out loud because it really is beyond astonishing: *"Planet.* This alien planet."

Mentally judging the rocket's size against the tiny chamber she woke up in, Ana slowly circles the craft. On either side of her door are two sealed portals. But as she comes around to the rear of the rocket, Ana stops short. There's *another door,* half open in the wind, with another mechanical staircase clawing on to the rocky soil.

Her heart leaps into her throat and she covers the ground in seconds. *I'm not alone here, not alone!* She's halfway up the stairs before she's even fully realized what she is doing.

She swings the door wide to . . .

Nothing.

The compartment is identical to hers, down to the grilled walkway and the black leather chair and the bright white light filling a space lined with red cushioned walls. But there's no sign of life, not even an indentation in the seat where a body might have rested. Ana steps all the way inside, and the heavy door falls shut behind her.

The disappointment crests like a wave, all hope and possibility of companionship slipping away in the undertow. She feels it roaring straight for her and immediately knows that if she lets it in, she will be paralyzed. She makes a split-second's decision: *No!*

Ana has no idea what kind of person she was, or *is*, but one thing she does know right now: Loneliness and self-pity are not only self-indulgent but dangerous. *You have now arrived on Paradox.* She's maybe alone, definitely damaged, possibly deranged—but she's *here*. On this alien planet.

She has no one to rely on but herself.

Ana turns back toward the door. As she starts to push it open, a sound outside makes her pause. It's a grinding noise, a *MRRROOOOAR* and a *GRRRRRRAH*, like a dozen bulldozers moving across torn-up ground. It's loud and harsh, digging into her ears like claws, like hungry things—and somehow Ana knows that whatever is out there, it's alive.

The walkway below her is shaking, and suddenly she's fighting to keep her balance; then the door whips out of her hand, and through the opening she sees a rush of brown like a moving mountain. There's a gust of stale air, then a bloodred maw and jagged teeth as tall as fence posts and a throat that goes down down down like a slide to hell.

Ana tumbles back onto the grille walkway. Her head

crashes against the footrest of the chair. The door bangs shut. Her left hand flies to her right hip with practiced fluidity, and suddenly there's a dagger in her hand.

Outside, the noise is a roar is a bellow is a dull throbbing moan and then gradually it's all but gone.

Long minutes tick by, uncounted except for the staccato rhythm of Ana's breath and the pounding of her heart. Still shaking all over, she finally sits up and drags herself to her feet. Her fingers tremble as she slides the dagger back into its sheath, trying to figure out how she managed to whip out a deadly weapon with all the ease of ripping open a candy bar. She explores her vest and discovers reinforced pockets containing a short-handled serrated blade and a slim steel pistol.

She's obviously more than ready, but for what? For that *thing*?

She stands up and puts both hands on the door handle. The continued silence outside, and the comforting bulk of her weapons, bolsters her courage. She thrusts the door open.

Nothing.

Just dust and dirt and watery sunlight, as far as her eyes can see. No slavering mouth, no nightmare monster waiting to pounce.

Ana feels a flicker of doubt. What *did* she see, exactly? She thinks of how recently she's woken up, thinks of her broken mind, all those memories she must have had that don't exist anymore. And now she's seeing monsters?

She rubs the back of her head and feels the tender spot

that's already rising into a lump where she slammed into the chair. Did she black out for a few seconds?

Squeezing her hands into fists, Ana starts down the narrow staircase as it rocks in the dust-heavy blasts of wind. She studies the landscape. It's empty—and desolate and untamed in a way that sharpens into a raw, spare kind of beauty. The vast basin she's in looks as if it's been scooped out of the sky. The cliff disappears into the distance off to the edges of her vision in both directions. Flat ground all the way, and a cliff on every edge. Ana is one tiny speck in a giant bowl-shaped crater.

The emptiness is overwhelming, but it's also reassuring. There's nowhere a creature that big could possibly hide.

It must have been just in my head.

The ground at the base of the stairs is firm under her feet. She bends down and presses her palm into it. Zigzag cracks run along its sun-warmed surface. Patches of thin, yellowish grass tuft up here and there. She traces one of the cracks with her finger. Is there water under the ground somewhere? The air is breathable, obviously, but how habitable is this place? *This planet.*

Ana circles the rocket and ducks underneath the staircase leading down from her door, moving toward a certain spot on the hull, moving toward something specific, though she has no idea what. She closes her eyes, and in her mind sees a spark, hears a loud *ting* of metal striking metal. When she opens her eyes, her palm rests flat on the side of the rocket at shoulder level. She slides her hand over.

17

A.

A single capital letter scratched into the red paint. *A for Ana.*

Is it juvenile to autograph what has to be a multimillion-dollar spaceship? Undoubtedly. Ana wonders what kind of person she was to be comfortable defacing equipment like this, but at the same time she can't suppress a smile. She didn't know, didn't remember any of this, but once again, her body did. It's just another sign that there is still hope for her past, however deeply it might be locked inside her.

Then something catches her eye that she'd missed the first time around. On the hull under the staircase is a keypad.

She considers the display. There are letter and number buttons, and a blank screen half the size of her hand that looks just like the fingerpad that unlocked the door to her compartment. The display tickles something she can't remember, but when she stops trying to see herself in the memory, the knowledge is suddenly there.

Ana's fingers dart over the keypad, tapping out a ten-digit sequence of letters and numbers; then she presses her index finger against the center of the screen. She holds it there for a moment, then pulls it away, and the mechanism begins to vibrate. With a chirp and a burble, the panel around the screen begins to shake.

She scrambles out of the way. For a second she has the panicked idea that this is the start sequence, that the rocket will take off without her and leave her stranded here on the planet. But then the rocket's base, right above the thrusters, splits open at the middle. Two wide drawers swing out in either direction.

The drawer closest to Ana contains a giant backpack, nearly as tall as she is. When she peers inside, she finds pockets bulging with all sorts of food and expeditionary supplies. The other drawer is empty, nothing but a hole as big as a broom closet. She thinks about the empty chamber above her, the unfurled staircase. Has her mystery companion been here, too? If so, where did he or she go?

With a sigh, Ana lifts her pack out of the drawer and rolls it onto the ground. The surprise and relief of finding something is gobbled up by the understanding of what her find actually means. It's like the notice at the end of a ride that says, *Goodbye! Come again soon!* Only far less cheerful. And without the *come again.* It's telling her she's going to be here on this planet for a good long time. The idea is a logical one—you don't cross space on a day trip, after all—and yet seeing this concrete proof brings reality crashing down on her. She's here, alone, for the foreseeable future. With no memory and no idea of what happens next.

Lifting her eyes to the horizon, Ana looks toward the distant cliff at the basin's edge. The wind gusts, blowing dirt into her eyes. As she brings her hand up to shield them, she hears a very faint *tick, tick, tick.* It's the same sound she noticed when she first woke up.

She slides up her sleeve. There's a band on her right wrist, a wide strap that's in the place where a watch would be—but it is very clearly not a watch. It's made of a slim, bendable pleather that's tight but not constricting. There's no face on the band, just a dark gummy portion that might be a screen. But the greater part of the band is taken up with a row of pale numbers that are moving and changing in time with the ticking—

00:26:43:02

00:26:43:01

The numbers are counting slowly down. Ana watches them, fascinated, registering immediately that they represent the seconds of her life, passing one by one.

00:26:43:00

00:26:42:59

00:26:42:58

She could almost swear she knows what this thing is for, but the knowledge is floating somewhere just outside her grasp. It's obviously a countdown—but to what? What happens after the almost-twenty-seven hours are up? She thinks back to the letter from the mysterious J. R. Pritchett. *Be mindful of the countdown*, it said.

Ana groans. Putting the puzzle aside for the moment, she studies the rest of her band—*circlet, that's what it's called*—running her fingers over the surface. She's not surprised when once again her fingers know just what to do.

She presses a finger into the center of the tiny screen and a pencil-thin beam of white light fountains up. The light diffuses into a prismatic rainbow stretching flat across the back of her hand. Etched in the light is a rough outline of a bare, rocky land with a cliff in the distance. She lifts her hand toward the horizon and discovers that the display exactly matches the land formations she sees ahead.

Now what?

Ana moves the fingers of her other hand into the band of light. She splays her fingers wide, then slowly draws them together in a pinching movement. *Zoom out,* she thinks.

Immediately the cliff in the display shrinks in size until she has a bird's-eye view of an oblong crater. There's even a label: CRANIUM. Right in the center is a flashing red point. Leading away from the point is a red-dotted line that crosses the Cranium and follows a path studded with labeled land formations: the DEAD FOREST; the high, rugged TIMOR MOUNTAINS; some kind of wide sandy stretch; then the banks of the MARAQA SEA. On the shore of the sea is a large red X.

A map. She's looking at a map, directions for her journey.

The rocket is planted right in the middle of the Cranium. By lining up the map-screen, Ana now knows exactly which direction she has to go.

21

Follow the preset path, the letter said. So here she has it.

Ana scans the land ahead of her and finds a landmark on the distant edge of the Cranium—a clump of reddish boulders that looks like a painted campfire from this distance. That will be her guidepost on this first leg of the journey.

She turns off her map display by pressing the little screen, just as smoothly as if she's done it a million times before. The numbers on the edge of the circlet are still ticking, counting down, and the knowledge makes her chest tighten. Twenty-six hours, and then what?

Experience, her instructions told her. *Discover. Survive.*

She doesn't know how she's going to do any of those things, but one thing's no longer a mystery: she knows where she's going, and she has a specific path to get there. For a girl with a gaping hole where her memory used to be, it feels like luxury indeed.

There's nothing left now but to get moving.

THREE

00:26:19:02

The pack towers over Ana like a second head, but once she has it firmly in place on her back, it's not nearly as heavy as it looked. She quickly settles into a brisk walking pace. The only tricky thing is the wind, which seems to think she's a kite and keeps trying to blow her away. Ana imagines herself puffing up and drifting—*up, up into the purple-pink sky*—imagines a long string anchoring her to the cracked earth. She twists her head around to look at the suns. The one overhead isn't that bright; it's like looking up at a fluorescent lightbulb. But the other sun is blazing. She's glad it's rising to her back, though at last glance it does seem to have edged slightly up on the horizon.

Tiny dark specks are dotted all across the sky—reverse

stars or something, like a mismatched X-ray of the universe. She wonders if one of those pinpricks off in the millions-of-miles-away distance is her own sun. She wonders if there are other people on this planet—and if any of them have their heads back, too, studying the sky.

At the waterfront, she reminds herself. *If there's anyone else living on the planet, that's where they'll be. At the red X.*

She walks.

Once, she thinks she hears a grinding sound in the distance, and she freezes in momentary panic. She thinks again of that roaring mouth, the horrible flash of brown lumpy body. *No. It wasn't real.* She settles the pack more firmly on her shoulders and walks on—

and on—

and on.

Minutes and hours fly away, but the crater's edge seems no nearer; only the constantly changing numbers on her circlet give her any sense of time and progress. And the lonely rocket, shrinking away behind her. Ana keeps her eyes on the distant crop of boulders, like her feet are on the imaginary dotted line, and trudges on.

Then, up ahead, something catches her eye. It's a sort of twinkling, *like speckled sunlight on a waterfall,* she thinks. *Like hundreds of tiny liquid mirrors.* Whatever it is, it's long and thin like a sheer scarf suspended in the air and carried along by the wind. Ana tries to go around it, but the backpack makes her clumsy, and for a second it's all she can do to keep her balance, and then—

Sssssssssss

The glittering strand of light slides over her body and covers her like the spray of a hot shower, like comfort, like coming home. She falls over some invisible edge and—

What a crazy, crazy day . . . it's gone by in a flash and my to-do list is longer than it was this morning. I'm bone-weary. Pushing up the white sleeve of my lab coat, I check my watch. Five forty-five! Already?

I can't wait to head home. Tonight is the last game of the playoffs, and Brian will be waiting. We said six o'clock for pizza, but I'll have to put him off until seven. At the earliest.

My eyes drift from my watch to my wedding ring—it still looks weird to see it there. I wonder if one day I'll be so used to it that I won't even notice. No way. It's too perfect. Like my life. Except for all this prion madness, of course; but we're so close now to figuring it out, and even if the worst happens . . . No. I won't let myself think of that. I just need to finish up here and get home.

The phone rings, and I snap back into work mode. I'll call Brian later, just as soon as I get a second to catch my breath. Scribbling a reminder on a yellow sticky note with my right hand, I grab the phone with my left.

"Yeah?"

"Bailey, what's keeping you?" It's Jackson, of course. "We haven't gotten the readouts yet. Are we getting any insight from the PX37 trials? Talk to me!"

Talk to him? Right, if he'd just shut up for a second. "Listen, Jackson, it's next on my list. I'm working on all cylinders here, but Tang is out with the flu and it's just me."

Jackson is silent for a moment.

"The flu?"

"That's all it is," I say. "Doctor's sworn statement. Tang will be back in tomorrow."

"Forget it," Jackson says. "Let him go. It's not worth the risk."

"But—"

"Damn it, Bailey, you of all people know what's at stake here! You wrote the report! Get rid of Tang and get me the information. I'm sending over some new tests that need to be run, too. Anticipation sensors and modulation adjustments. We have to figure out what's out of place."

"But I—"

"Readouts, on my desk. I need you on this for as long as it takes."

And he's gone, leaving me glaring down at the receiver like I could vaporize it with a look. I groan, lean my head forward, and hide behind my hair for just a second. So much for the playoffs and pizza with Brian. I reach over to hang up the phone—

Gasping, Ana finds herself facedown on the ground, her cheek pressing against the hard-packed dirt, pinned by her backpack's heavy weight. She struggles to a sitting position, rubbing her cheek and feeling the fine imprint of the rocky soil on her skin.

What just happened?

Wincing at a throbbing pain in her temples, she turns and looks behind her. The gossamer strand of light is twisting away, but it seems smaller now, and fainter. As she watches, one little mirror at a time blows away like dandelion puffs on the wind until soon there's nothing left.

Nothing but the memory of what she saw.

Ana looks at her hands, the sleeve of her coarse gray jump-suit, and her tan fingers, plain and unadorned, and sees again the creamy skin from the vision and the shimmer of the dia-mond ring as she turned it from side to side. There were yel-low curls tumbling over her shoulders . . . Ana reaches up and touches short-cropped hair along her scalp, shorter than the length of her fingers, so short she doesn't even know what color it is.

But she's almost sure it's not blond.

The experience she just dropped into, or lived, or whatever that was—it felt as real to her as everything she's felt since leaving the rocket. It's rock solid. And yet . . .

That wasn't me. I could swear to it.

But then who was it?

Maybe there is a settlement somewhere on this planet, and some trick of the atmosphere is projecting these strands out into space. But strands of what . . . experience? Memory? Mental projection?

Or maybe the real Bailey lived somewhere millions of light-years away; maybe that strand came the way of the stars, top-pling head over tail to land on her through some quirk of time and space.

Ana has no way of knowing. And somehow, she is not en-tirely sure that she *wants* to know. For now, this experience is hers, and she hangs it in the empty closet of her mind like a memory of her very own, like the first fancy dress in a ward-robe she thought might be empty forever.

As she gets to her feet and walks on, she thinks about how

real those moments felt—even more real, somehow, than her present. There's an ache inside her, a longing for the fullness of Bailey's world, however briefly visited.

Jackson, she thinks, scowling. And *Brian*, with a smile for her own bare fingers. She replays the scenario over and over, the thoughts keeping her company in the emptiness of her own mind as the minutes tick away.

At long last she approaches the crater wall. Looking at her circlet, she sees it's been two hours since she left the rocket. The overhead sun is pretty much in the same position as when she first started out, while the brighter sun has fully risen and is inching upward into the sky.

Inside her jumpsuit, Ana's body is slippery with sweat. She pauses to let the wind cool her down as she considers the cliff wall. It towers above her, at least twenty-five feet high. She notices herself gauging the crevices and footholds scattered across the rock face—apparently, she has some familiarity with rock climbing—but those spots are few and far between. The thought doesn't trouble her; instead she feels a quickening of excitement in her chest at the prospect of the climb.

Interesting.

Ana shrugs off her pack and lays it flat on the ground. The pack has a wide buckle on the front, and when she unlatches it, the whole thing unfolds into a T-shape, the heavy nylon frame bulging with pockets. Each compartment is labeled: CLIMBING GEAR. BEDROLL. INFLATABLE RAFT. FIRST AID. VITALS.

She opens VITALS to find packets upon packets of food:

macaroni-and-cheese; butter wafers; desiccated goat cheese; dried tropical fruit mix. There's a large squishy tube that must be a collapsed water bottle. But where will she find water to fill it?

The thought makes her throat burn. Then she sees a pocket labeled WATER. Inside are hundreds of pill packets. She pulls out a handful. The packaging is plain silver, unlabeled except for a small ID number in the corner of each packet. She juggles the packets in her hand for a moment and then thinks, *Why not?* If she doesn't have water, she's dead anyway. It's worth a try.

She punches out a tablet no bigger than her thumbnail and pops it into her mouth.

At first there's nothing. Then she feels a fizzing on her tongue, then—*ooooh*, it's like a fountain opens inside her mouth . . . a fountain of stale, artificial water, true, but for this second it's the best thing she's ever tasted. And it's just enough; it fills her mouth but doesn't overflow. She puffs her cheeks a little to hold it all in, swirls it around inside her mouth, and then swallows.

Dried water, she muses. Maybe the Ana she can't remember would see this as an everyday occurrence. Maybe that Ana turned on a faucet and little white pills came tumbling out into her cup. Somehow, she doesn't think so. But right now they are just what she needs, and that's more than good enough.

She sits and leans back against the crater wall, thinking it's probably a good idea to rest a moment, countdown or not.

She could use some time to really study the map, figure out how she's going to travel all that distance, think through a better plan than the slapdash thrown-together one she has now, which is nothing more than: *Don't think. Keep moving!*

Make a plan, then follow it through. In some deep core of herself, Ana knows that's how she works best. She can even see the quick flash of a ballpoint pen scribbling *Things to Do* on a fresh sheet of lined paper, another non-memory gusting around in her sinkhole of a mind. So, planning. And recharging.

Then she hears it.

The sound is faint at first, like something on the edge of her imagination, but that *MRRROOOOAR* is not something that can be mistaken for anything else. In a second Ana is on her feet, hand over her eyes to block the glare.

If the sound is real, then the mouth was real, and the whole brown monster-body-creature along with it.

This time, the noise doesn't dissipate when she stops to listen. It gets louder. At first she can't tell where it's coming from, but then she sees a cloud of dust in the distance, puffing and rolling along the ground.

It's headed in her direction.

Reassembling her pack and hoisting it onto her back, Ana spins around to face the crater wall. There's a crack in the rock face just out of reach, and farther up she can see a few workable handholds. It will have to be good enough.

A quick glance over her shoulder shows that the thing is

nearer already, like a storm cloud closing in, loud and growing louder. How does it cover ground so fast? At this rate, it'll be on her in fifteen or twenty minutes. Maybe less.

Ana turns back to the wall. With some kind of practiced motion she gives a little jump and just reaches the crack, jamming her fingers into place and bracing her toes against the rock face. She pulls up hard, stretches her right leg up to reach the next crevice, shifts, and climbs again. The rock is solid for the most part, but little cascades of pebbles skitter down in her wake, and the higher she goes, the more precarious her position feels. Any exhilaration she might have felt at the climb is canceled out by the beast behind her. The minutes slip away to the pounding beat of her heart as she scales the sheer rock face, another leg up, another too-small hole to stuff her fingers into. Just barely making it. Just barely is enough. Until finally, she's nearly to the top.

Behind her, the roar is now deafening. How close is that thing? How long since she started her climb? She doesn't want to look, but she can't help it. Just a quick glance over her shoulder—

Long white teeth raging out of a cloud of reddish-brown dust.

Swallowing a shriek, Ana turns back to the wall and sees a root hanging over the top of the cliff face. With no time to test its strength, she grabs hold of it, shifting all her weight onto the growth in one desperate tug.

In a shower of dirt and pebbles, the root slowly loosens,

pulling away from the rock wall. *No!* The dust cloud gusts behind her, buffeting her and coating her like sea spray—like a giant's breath.

Her feet are still jammed into the wall, but both hands are around the unstable root and she's tilting backward, rapidly losing her balance.

Ana feels herself begin to slip.

FOUR

00:23:22:59

Then a sharp sound cuts through the roar: "Here! Grab this!"

What? Ana looks up, squinting straight into the overhead sun. There's something right above her head. A hand?

"Come on!"

With a desperate lunge, Ana grabs the outstretched hand— and is pulled over the lip of the crater.

She scrambles to her feet to find a boy standing in front of her. She's so shocked to find herself facing another person that at first, all she can do is stare. He's tall, with light shaggy hair, maybe in his late teens or a little older. *Around my age,* she thinks, then wonders how old she *is.*

"Thank you," she gasps, almost a reflex, and yet it feels like a vast understatement.

The boy nods, but all his attention is down in the crater. The ground shakes as the creature pounds itself against the cliff wall. Standing well back from the edge and leaning forward, Ana gets her first good look. It appears to be some kind of giant monstrous worm. It has a huge lumpy head and a long dirt-colored body that disappears into a cloud of dust.

"But what is it *doing* here?" the boy mutters.

Ana turns to look at him more closely. He's wearing a gray jumpsuit with a black vest, sturdy hiking boots, a towering backpack. Ana's heartbeat quickens.

"The rocket," she says, suddenly getting it. "The open door. You were in that other compartment!"

He turns and looks at her, an odd expression on his face.

"I'm Ana," she says quickly.

"Ana," he says, his smile tentative, as if she's a strange puzzle he's trying to figure out. "I'm Todd."

The earth trembles under them again, and Ana steps farther back from the edge. The boy—Todd—shudders. "I'm sorry," he says. "That creature freaks me out. I can't figure out what it's doing here."

"But you did come on the rocket?"

Todd nods. She doesn't remember him, of course, no more than she does anything else in her life, but something about the way his hair hangs across his forehead has the unexpected *ping* of familiarity.

Ana smiles awkwardly. "Sorry. I'm—well, I've got some memory issues. Surgical retrograde amnesia. That's what my letter said. I have no personal memories at all. Just basic knowledge and some muscle memory, though I don't seem to have any trouble with keeping new memories. I can remember everything since I woke up on the rocket."

Todd is silent for a second, then says, "I guess I have the same condition. My first memory is waking up in the rocket." He raises his left arm, pulls down his sleeve, and flashes his own circlet at her. Ana can see the numbers on his band moving. "I know we're here from Earth. We're supposed to follow the map and reach the colony on the shores of Maraqa. That's about it."

"Maybe the memory wipe is standard procedure," Ana says, but she can't suppress a stab of disappointment. There was a moment when she'd thought this might be her chance at getting some insight into who she is and why she's here. On the other hand, things are no worse than they were an hour ago—in fact, they're quite a bit better. She has a companion, and two broken minds have to be better than one.

"We ought to keep moving," she says, glancing down at her circlet. "Twenty-three hours sounds like ages, but I have a feeling—"

There's a crack like thunder, and the edge of the crater wall collapses, the ground dropping away beneath Ana's feet. For a second she's part of a cascading rockslide; then Todd grabs her backpack and pulls her free.

"We need to put some distance between us and that thing," Todd says.

"No kidding," Ana says. "Let's go!"

Todd sets a brisk, steady pace, his boots kicking up puffs of dusty soil. His purposeful strides make it clear he knows where he's going, but he hasn't activated his map. "You know the way from here?" Ana asks.

He nods. "I pulled it up just a few minutes ago. There aren't a lot of different path options at this point."

They are following a narrow, dusty path that winds through the rugged landscape for a mile or two before disappearing into a dark bank of trees: the Dead Forest, which dominates the near horizon. Beyond the forest, the Timor Mountains stand like a row of sentinels blocking their view of the sea. Ana thinks back to her own bird's-eye view of the route. Todd is right. There's just one way to go forward.

"Something else, though," he says. He glances at her sideways. "This amnesia? I'm not sure how it is for you, but I do seem to know certain things about this planet—the terrain, the landscape, facts. You know?" He looks anxious, as if he's begging her to tell him his condition makes some kind of sense.

"It sounds a little like my muscle memory," Ana says. "My body does its own thing sometimes, before my mind even catches on."

"Who knows how this stuff works?" he says.

Ana feels a grin pulling at the sides of her mouth. A word comes to her: *schadenfreude*, and her mind fills in the blank: *feeling joy at someone else's suffering.* That's not exactly what this is, but knowing that her new companion is just as broken as she is makes the uncertainty and emptiness of their situation some-how easier to bear.

The path is little more than a faint trail in the rocky soil, with sparse, coarse vegetation that looks nothing like Earth grass. It's wild and untamed, but just the fact that it's bona fide plant life, here on this alien planet, is pretty amazing. As they walk, the worm's grinding and pounding grows fainter until eventually it fades altogether. Then it's just silence and rough terrain and a bright pink sky overhead. Just a boy and a girl out for a casual afternoon stroll.

Or so Ana tries to tell herself.

"I'm sorry for taking off on you back at the rocket," Todd says after a few minutes.

"Don't be," Ana says. "How could you even know I was there? I wasn't expecting you, either."

He tilts his head and studies her, seeming to come to a decision. "Still. It's a rough world out here. We'll be better off sticking together."

Together. Now there's an interesting word. She'd resigned herself to being fully alone for this journey, and while she's thrilled to be proven wrong, that core of self-reliance remains. Another behavioral muscle memory, perhaps? Still, if they're going to be companions, they should try to find some way to connect. But can two people really get to know each other when neither of them properly know themselves? "Tell me everything you remember," she says. "Whatever's there, start to finish."

The story Todd tells is nearly identical to her own: circlet, letter, mission, map-with-dotted-direction-line, and all. The only difference in their stories lies in her early introduction to the worm. Ana grimaces. They can't build a shared past, that's clear. But maybe, going forward *together*, they can jointly make some sense of right now. "So here we are," she says. "Twin amnesiacs off exploring an alien world."

Todd grins and it's like a sunrise breaking over his pale face, triggering again that indefinable quickening inside her chest, that reaching for . . . *something*. Ana finds herself suddenly needing to look away. "So back to the memory-loss thing," she says.

"What about it?"

"Don't you wonder what the deal is?" she asks. "Why would whoever's in charge of this expedition send us to an alien planet with no memories? What possible advantage could there be?"

Todd's eyebrows come together as he shakes his head. "I don't know. I suppose we'll have to figure it out as we go along." He clears his throat.

Ana keeps her expression steady, but inwardly she wishes she had half the chilled-out temperament Todd seems to possess. He looks so much more comfortable with his condition than she is.

On the other hand, why *should* she be comfortable with this? Having a blank, empty mind is not natural, it's not right, and—sure, for now all she can do is take things as they are. But one thing's certain: If there are any answers to be had anywhere on this planet, she's going to find them.

Whatever it takes.

The scenery stays stubbornly the same as the trail winds on—an endless display of flat, barren earth with scattered and struggling vegetation. It's like a world that used to have life and is clinging desperately to what little is left. Overhead and to their rear, the twin suns smolder in the bright sky.

As they walk, Ana catches herself more than once following the curve of Todd's shoulder, her gaze lingering at the hollow of his throat before she jerks her attention away. What is going on with her? She wishes she could blame this on muscle memory, like her eyes are used to lingering on Todd. But she's pretty sure it doesn't work that way. Still . . .

"I think we knew each other before," she says suddenly.

Todd jumps a little, then says, "Well, we did come in the same rocket."

"I know. It just . . ." She can't express that flare of *knowing* she gets every time she looks at him. "It seems like something more than that. I don't know. I'm probably crazy."

Todd shifts his pack around on his back. "Do you want to take a few minutes' rest?" he asks. "We've been going for an hour straight, maybe more. Whatever that creature was, it's long gone by now."

Ana frowns, and her eyes flick to her circlet. "What about the countdown? Don't we need to keep moving?"

Todd casts an uncertain look at the trail ahead of them. "Yeah, I guess," he says.

Ana frowns. "Got anything more than that?"

"What?"

"Well, you said you know stuff about this place," Ana says. "So what happens when the timer hits zero? Do you know?"

He's already shaking his head. "Not exactly . . ."

But something's making him jumpy, and the idea that he might know more than he's saying is suddenly too much. "Come on," she snaps. "You obviously know something. This timer, all these seconds ticking away and toward *what*? Death? Life? Destruction? Dinner?"

Todd grins, then seems to catch himself, and his face goes serious again. "Okay, this is what I do know. You've noticed the movement of the suns, right?"

Ana squints at the sky. "Sure. The bright one seems to be doing all the moving so far."

"Torus," Todd says. "That's the brighter sun. Its orbital period takes about a day on-planet. We're in a binary star system, of course, but Anum, up there"—he motions to the steady overhead orb—"moves much more slowly. You can hardly track it with the naked eye. I think Anum's orbital period takes about a year."

"Okay," Ana says, "thanks for the astronomy bulletin, but—"

"But," he interrupts, "once each day—the middle of the day, I guess it would be considered—Torus passes directly in Anum's path. It's called the sunsmeet, and we *don't* want to be outside for it."

"That's it? That's the big countdown, some kind of eclipse?"

Todd frowns. "It's more than just an eclipse. The solar

40

response is fierce and dangerous. Trust me, we need to get to the colony by zero hour, before the sunsmeet."

Ana nearly stops walking. "Wait, a colony?"

Todd nods, turning to continue down the narrow path. Head spinning, Ana turns to follow him. But as she thinks about it, she realizes there's an echo of recognition around the word. It fits. They're headed for a settlement on this planet, where they will find safety.

This bit of knowledge warms her as she follows Todd down the narrow path. The countdown has shifted from a threatening specter to a friendly cheerleader. *Keep going!* the glowing numbers seem to chant. *Just reach your destination and everything will be okay!*

And something else: a colony means people, people who will know what's going on, who maybe can even fix their memories—or who can at least fill in the gaps. Relief ripples through her.

Then they step around a bend and her feeling of relief slips away. About a half mile ahead the path dips down a shallow incline, then leads straight into a bank of trees so dense it looks like an impassable wall.

The Dead Forest.

They've been making their way toward it for hours, but now that they're right here, she can't believe it looks so . . . dead. Ana shivers. *A name is just a name, right?* But its still, silent look, the dark cast of the shadows between the trees, sets her nerves on edge. Something in there isn't right.

On the path ahead of her, Todd has stopped walking. Ana thinks back to his earlier hesitation, of how he knows the landscape. . . .

"This is what you've been nervous about, isn't it?" she asks.

When he turns toward her, though, there is a look of purpose in his eyes. "We've got to go through it," he says. "There's no other way. It's just a forest."

She decides to ignore the slight tremor in his voice. "Just a forest," she repeats, surprising herself by reaching out and giving Todd's hand a quick squeeze. The touch of his skin makes her suddenly remember Bailey's hands, her sparkling ring, and she finds herself glancing around, looking for a shimmer. But there are no floating distractions here, just the ever-present suns and the Dead Forest looming ahead.

"Let's do this," she says.

They stride on toward the forest.

"So," he says after a moment, looking at her slyly, "you got any memory of Sixteen Questions rattling around in that mind of yours?"

The shift in tone jars Ana, but then she realizes she *does* remember it. A complicated back-and-forth game of nested questions. Has she always hated this game, or is that just her imagination? She narrows her eyes. "Are you trying to distract me from the bastion of evil that's up ahead?"

Todd grins as he brushes his hair out of his face. "I'll take that as your first Q. Since yes-and-no answers are not accepted in this round, I'm going to reply with: In addition to providing a positive distraction from the forthcoming uncertainty, does the game of Sixteen Questions activate any dormant memories of your past?"

Ana's mind races. Maybe she hated this game once, but Todd's right. The distraction and the challenge have her pulse racing like she's back in the presence of that monster worm. Except this adrenaline rush is all good, and all hers.

"My mind is unfortunately empty of any and all specific memories," she says, shaping each word carefully, seeing how she can turn this game to her advantage, "and this mind wants to know what *your* mind knows about the existence of that monster that was chasing us back there."

Todd's face darkens. "It's not supposed to be here," he mutters.

Ana swallows. Back on the cliff, she heard him say something similar. He's slipping out of his Sixteen Questions persona, but she feels no need to push back. "Go on," she says.

"None of the planet scans of Paradox showed any signs of animal life. None at all. There *was* evidence that millions of years ago, a giant wormlike creature used to roam the planet. But it's long extinct. So why is it here now?"

"Planet scans?" Ana says incredulously. "How do you know about that?"

Todd grimaces. "I told you. I know stuff about this place. Physical things. I just think about it and the knowledge is there."

Ana nods. "Well, maybe the creature is a different life form entirely? Maybe it escaped the scans that way?"

Todd's already shaking his head. "It wasn't here," he insists.

43

"And then the first thing I thought of when I saw it was *Vermiletum*. But no, that would be ridiculous."

Vermi letum. Deadly worm. Apparently her former life included some Latin. "What do you mean, *Vermiletum?*" she asks. "You've seen that thing somewhere before, or heard of it?"

"Not really. I . . ." Todd flushes. "I just thought it triggered something, but . . . no."

There he goes again. He knows something, something he's too afraid to talk about. What could be more fearsome than a giant worm? *Vermiletum*. Something about that name fits. And what's more, the word stirs her up inside and sets her pulse pounding in her ears.

She has no idea why, but it makes her want to fight.

Her left hand crosses over to her hip and strokes the handle of the dagger resting in its sheath. An image flashes through her mind and she sees a gleaming blade hurtling through the air, turning end over end to sink with a satisfying *thunk* into a plywood target.

She's jerked back to the moment as Todd stops walking and turns, looking straight at her. His eyes are wide and staring, startlingly blue in his chalky face. "Forget the worm," he says, a little hoarsely. "It's all wrong. We just have to get to the end of the countdown, and to do that we've got to stay away from it, okay?"

Ana frowns. "I'm not going looking for it, but it makes sense to investigate as much as we can while we're here. What about the letter? Experience, discover, blah blah. If it shows up again, if it attacks . . . Do you suppose we could kill it if we had to, if we worked together? Maybe stabbed or shot it in just the right spot?"

"No!" Todd barks. "The worm is something else." He turns his back on her and sets off down the path again. "Just trust me, okay? It's more than it seems. As bad as it looks, the worm is even worse. You don't want to get anywhere near it."

Ana closes her eyes a moment and flashes back to that slavering jaw, those rows of jagged teeth. The thing is like a tank—sixteen tanks strung end to end. What does she really think a couple of kids with pistols and knives could do against it? She was told to experience and discover, sure. She was also told to survive.

But the rush of adrenaline now coursing through her body is something else altogether. Because she's discovered something hard inside her, something cold and strong and razor-sharp. There is solid iron at her core. She will not break, will not bend, will not deviate from whatever path she embarks upon. And right now she knows with deadly certainty that she will do whatever it takes to defeat that worm.

Or die trying.

After Successful Test Mission, Manned Paradox Expedition Imminent

Galaxy Voice

The first unmanned space probes fitted with neo-Alcubierrean warp drives have successfully completed their maiden voyage, reaching Paradox in a record four months. The tiny planet, which upon its discovery a decade ago was named Cyclid-Bf, quickly became a public fixation due to its abundant Earth-like qualities. "It's got it all—ample groundwater, ideal surface temperature, breathable atmosphere," said Dr. Alan Bartleby, astrophysicist and Paradox expert. "Soil analysis and planet scans have shown it fully capable of supporting life." No animal life has been detected on the planet, though fossilized remains suggest the existence of intelligent life forms dating back millions of years. "It's like Earth 2.0," said Dr. Bartleby. "All systems are focused on getting us there as soon as possible."

Tuesday's successful probe landing now brings the planet within the range of manned space expeditions in the foreseeable future. "It's only a matter of time," said Alisha LeBewh of Savitech Corp. "We've got funding and sponsors lining up, and a list of candidates a mile long. Now that technology has caught up with discovery, we can finally take steps toward breaking through that final frontier."

FIVE

At the threshold of the Dead Forest, the path winds down a few hundred feet, then disappears into the solid wall of trees.

"There's something about this place," Ana whispers. She glances at Todd. Despite his determined stride, Ana can see tension in the set of his neck, in his rigid posture. She can almost feel the fear coursing through him.

"What is it?" she says.

"The forest?" Todd shrugs, then ruins the effect with a nervous swallow. "It's fine. No big deal."

"Come on, Todd," she says, pushing past him. The barren ground makes way for little tufts of yellowish growth, and bushes claw their way up out of the ground as they near the trees. Ana is so busy studying the ground that she almost

47

misses the moment where the shift happens—but there's one step and then the next and suddenly it's as if she were inside a shuttered room. She's crossed over into the forest.

The trees loom overhead, so high she can't see where their canopies end, and so close together that the light's almost completely blocked out. The sunlight that does filter down is dim and watery. Each tree is nearly as wide around as the rocket she traveled here in. Six of her could probably hold hands in a circle and not reach around to the other side of just one trunk.

Stranger still, the trees aren't brown, and they aren't covered in bark. There are no leaves. In fact, there's no green anywhere.

Everything in the forest, every tree trunk and branch, is ash gray.

The Dead Forest. *Well, that makes sense.*

Suddenly she realizes she's alone. She looks back to see Todd standing just outside the tree line, silhouetted against the light. He's half leaning against a trunk, as though trying to persuade himself to keep moving forward. Ana feels a rush of sympathy for his obvious struggle. Then his jaw hardens and a steely look comes into his eyes. He marches forward, pushing into the trees at last. Ana moves aside as he walks past her and down the path.

As Ana starts to follow him, something on the ground catches her eye. She stops and squats down. At first glance the forest floor looks as if it's covered in dirt, but up close she sees that it's ash—a fine, gunmetal-gray powder.

She reaches toward the nearest tree and brushes its stony surface with the lightest touch. It's cold as ice. She flattens her palm against the rough surface, which is crisscrossed with dozens of little ridges. If she closes her eyes, she could almost trick herself into thinking she's got her hand on an Earth tree—but the moment she opens them again, it's abundantly clear that this is not the case. Each tree in this forest is like a giant fossil, a memory of something that used to be, something that's dead and gone and doesn't even know it.

Sliding her hand off the tree, she looks at her soot-blackened palm. It's thick with a dark powdery coating—like ash, but heavier—particles that cling to her skin. She rubs her hand against her jumpsuit and spreads a black ashy patch onto the cloth, but when she looks at her hand again, it shows little difference.

What is this stuff? Ana shudders.

This Dead Forest . . . somehow it feels *undead*. She looks around nervously and feels weirdly claustrophobic, as if she's suddenly stepped inside a dark haunted house with no exit.

Ana shakes herself. Where did *that* come from? Of course there's an exit—the path is clearly visible through the gloom— and *okay*, yes, it gets gloomier the farther in you go, but that doesn't mean there's no end. The dotted line of their map will take care of that.

"Todd?" she calls, suddenly realizing that he's no longer in sight.

Jumping up, Ana adjusts her pack and starts to run,

remembering the jittery, fearful way Todd took off. What if he's left the path? What if she can't find him?

But then she turns a corner and runs smack into him.

Todd is standing in the middle of the trail, not moving a muscle. She comes around him and gasps. His eyes are glazed, his mouth slightly open. Ana grabs his arm, her fear disappearing in the palpable sense of his own. "Come on, Todd. Let's go."

Todd shakes himself, obviously trying to break free from whatever's got hold of him, but not quite succeeding. Could it be some kind of panic attack? Nerves?

"You didn't tell me you had forest issues," she continues with forced lightness, leading him along the path. "Though I probably should have guessed from all those clues you were dropping earlier. Anything you want to talk about?"

"No . . . issues," he says, but each word seems to take effort, as if it's being dragged out of him.

"Don't worry," she says. "We'll just get through this and then you'll be okay."

"Must be . . . some kind of subconscious . . ." He's sweating now, tiny drops barely visible above his hairline.

Ana's still pulling him along, but it's getting more difficult, as if his feet want to root themselves to the ground.

". . . aversion . . ."

His face is shiny with sweat and his eyes look glassy again. *What is going on?*

A twinge of panic starts somewhere in Ana's gut, because

it's suddenly clear that Todd's problem is much bigger than just a forest phobia. Should they turn around? No, they *have* to go through the forest. It's the only way to get where they're going.

Ana reaches over and grabs the circlet on Todd's left wrist. With a quick stroke she pulls up the map, which gleams against their dark backdrop. There's a flash of near-recognition in Todd's eyes as he tries to focus on the display.

"Hey, Todd," Ana says. "You see that? Gotta follow the directions. We're almost there."

They're not almost there—not as far as she can tell from the map, anyway. She clicks it off again and they move on. She wishes she could take the time to zoom out and get an idea of how far in they are and how far there is to go, but she's got all her focus on keeping Todd moving forward.

More and more it's looking like a battle she might not win.

"No!" she yells aloud at the thought. Todd jumps at the abrupt sound, then sinks back to his walk-be-dragged-shuffle. But that jump gives her an idea.

Ana stops and drops his arm, pausing for a second to catch her breath. As she does, she can see Todd's body beginning to shift, as if his very bones were pulling toward the ground. And she could swear she sees tendrils rising from the ground, little shoots twining around his heels, curling over the rims of his boots.

"It's so dark in here," he whispers. His voice is weirdly hollow, almost like it's disconnected from his body. His eyes are wide and staring and he's craning his head from side to side, but he doesn't seem to see her.

"Todd!" she says. But he doesn't even register her words. It's as if he's caught in the grip of some hallucination and isn't able to pull out of it. She's going to need some extreme measures.

She lifts his arms out in front of him. Todd is so gone he lets her, leaving his arms suspended in midair, like a mannequin or a zombie or whatever it is he's turning into. She activates his circlet map again and lines it up so that it's clear and sharp and right in front of him. Then she pulls back her arm and slaps him hard across the face. At the same time she yells, "RUN, TODD! RUN! Get out of here! You have to GO GO GO GO GO GO!"

It works like an electric shock. He vaults forward and starts tearing down the path, the roots and grasping tendrils falling away behind him. Ana stays right at his heels, giving him a shove if he slows, letting out another yell every so often, until her voice becomes a croak and her lungs are ready to explode and her feet are two leaden clumps that want to fall right off her legs.

Still they run on.

Ana's ears are full of a dark whispering rustle as they push through the forest, a rustle in a forest with no leaves, where the only living things are the two humans crashing through branches that grasp at them from faceless trunks.

Faster and faster they push on, over fallen trunks, under low limbs, across shallow, ashy streambeds. Spiky branches lash at her and a steady warm trickle starts down the side of her face, but she doesn't let herself stop.

If she stops, she knows she won't be able to start again.

When Ana thinks she can't run another step, she sees their goal up ahead. It's barely visible through the thinning tops of the trees, but it's there all right, bathed in the light of the double suns—the crest of a rocky slope. She can't pull up her own map or zoom out Todd's, which is bobbing like a carrot in front of a madly chasing donkey, but the Timor Mountain range begins just beyond the forest, and if they're now in sight, then there's still hope.

There's still hope.

SIX

00:19:06:44

Ana and Todd erupt from the forest, boots outstretched, arms flung to either side, like a couple of interstellar desperadoes escaping certain death and living to tell about it, somehow, against all odds.

It's been just a few hours since they entered the forest, but already Ana was forgetting the way the breeze could tickle and the light could tease, and forgetting, almost, the incomparable freedom of the open arc of the sky. Even the twin suns in their orbits beam down on her now like old friends. She thinks that even though she was running back in the forest, even though no roots were hooking her into the ground, still some part of her didn't fully return to life until she came back out into the open air.

Ana drops to her hands and knees on the soft ground, her heart going like a jackhammer, pounding a double-time beat.

At first she thinks it's just in its contrast that the planet suddenly looks so much more hospitable. But then she sees it's more than that: on this side of the forest, there is some serious plant life—the first healthy signs of growth she's seen on Paradox so far. Just ahead there's a little meadow with bluish-green grass and a few flowers. Small bushes and trees dot the sloping terrain, and more grass stretches out to the edge of her vision, off to the base of the high mountain peaks.

She squints up at Todd, who stands a little ahead of her. He's turned his map off and is hunched over, hands on his knees, taking big, gulping breaths. His eyes are full of all the right things—pain and fear and shame and anger—all those real, hard-to-bear human emotions.

"Hey," she says, pulling herself into a sitting position on the grass.

He walks back over and drops down beside her. "What happened in there? Do I even want to know?"

Ana considers this. "Probably not. But I think it's safe to say that you don't like forests too much."

Todd's mouth turns down, and Ana adds quickly, "Okay, it's actually more than that. Something's not right in that forest—there's something heavy and oppressive. I couldn't wait to get out of there myself. But it was more for you; almost as though some force in there had it out for you in particular."

Todd turns toward her, about to say something, and then he raises his eyebrows. "What did you do to yourself?" he says, looking at her forehead. He immediately starts burrowing in his pack.

Ana touches her right temple and discovers a warm, sticky dampness. She winces. "I'm fine," she says. "Must have been one of those branches I ran into. It's just a scratch."

"Still," he says, turning toward her with a small tube in one hand and a white cloth in the other. She grits her teeth as he wipes at the wound, then there's a cool pressure as he applies some gel from the tube.

"Peri-skin," he says, replacing the cap and sliding the tube back into his pack. "It'll set in a few seconds. You can probably tell the difference already."

Reaching her hand back up, Ana gingerly assesses the smooth, rubbery coating.

"Thanks," she says. She knows the peri-skin will anesthetize, disinfect, and fully repair her cut in hours, if not less.

Todd leans forward and touches a finger to her temple, and there's something in his look that makes Ana freeze. She swallows, suddenly uncomfortable. "What about you?" she asks. "How are you feeling?"

The change of subject works. Todd drops his hand and gets to his feet. "I'm fine," he says. "Come on. We can talk more as we walk, if you're doing all right. There's a plateau up here where we can take a real break."

"There is?"

Todd nods. "I saw it on the map. It's not far."

He reaches into a pocket of his vest and pulls out a handful of water capsules. He tosses her a couple and she catches them gratefully, punching one out and popping it in her mouth. Instantly refreshed, she revels in the feel of the water pouring down her dry throat.

She shoves the leftover tablets in her pocket, hears them rustle up against the folded letter. The letter! She runs the words over in her mind again. *Our world is on the brink of disaster. Your mission must succeed.* But what *is* the mission? And how can you succeed when you don't have any idea what you're supposed to be doing, much less how to do it?

Ana decides that, though they do need a break, it won't be a long one. There's too much ground to cover and too much that's still unknown.

Adjusting her pack, she follows Todd up the grassy slope. Above them looms the Timor range. The mountains look huge from here, so near they seem to be carved right out of the brilliant sky.

Ana looks sideways at Todd as they walk. He's definitely back in the land of the living, but something has changed between them. She feels a new strength as she strides next to him, shoulder to shoulder. She has no idea if they knew each other in a former life before their memories were scrubbed like a couple of old dinner plates. But this feels right, pushing forward together, following the map. Heading for the plateau, then on to the mountains.

Even as she thinks this, her stance is shifting and her gaze is narrowing and a flutter starts in her chest. She thinks back to the rush she got from her brief scale up the cliff face, and she suddenly knows that mountains are part of some love affair from her past. Maybe somewhere in her lost memory is an experience that will guide her. But for now she just knows this: she can't wait to get started climbing.

"That one's a volcano," Todd says, motioning to the peak directly in their path. "Mount Fahr."

Ana sniffs the air. That explains the faint sulfurous smell. Now that she's looking for it, she can see tendrils of steam curling from the peak. It looks steep for a volcano, at least by Earth standards. It's all rough hew and harsh angles. "Is it active?" she asks.

Todd shakes his head. "It's on a slow burn pattern. Should be safe enough."

Ana activates her circlet and lines up the map. The Timor range carves a long wedge across the face of the planet, guarding the way to the sea. There's no way to go around it. And the peaks on either side of Mount Fahr glower down like hulking giants. The volcano suddenly looks very climbable. It's the obvious choice.

"Okay," she says, but inwardly she's all smiles. *Bring on the climb!*

They reach the plateau a few minutes later, the wide-open space dotted with a couple of flat boulders. Ana lets her pack slide off her back and drops it near the closest stone. After carrying her pack all this time, taking it off is like ripping away some part of her, but it's no pain and all pleasure, a shot of pure joy. For a second, she feels so light she might float away.

Then tiredness sweeps over her and she collapses onto the boulder. It's long and flat and warm from the sunslight, with enough room for Ana to stretch out on her back with her knees steepled up and her boots propped on the edge. She folds her arms across her eyes and sinks onto the surface of the rock, her muscles loosening and settling on the stone. She lies there for long minutes, soaking up the quiet.

After a while she moves her arms and looks up at the sky and the pale sun, Anum. She imagines it meeting with Torus in a cataclysmic burst at zero hour. *Sunsmeet*, Todd called it. For now, at least, there are huge swaths of pink sky between the suns, though they are closer than when she first left the rocket. There are seventeen hours' worth of distance left between them, apparently. *And then what, exactly?*

Ana shivers and sits up.

Todd is standing with his back to her, looking back at the Dead Forest. His broad back is set and his feet are planted wide apart on the rocky ledge. Only his hair tosses up and down in the breeze.

"Hey," Ana says.

Todd lets out a sigh, his whole posture drooping a little, as if he's resigning himself to something he can't quite escape. "It happened the summer I was eight," he says.

His voice is barely more than a whisper. Ana pushes herself up the rest of the way, straining to make out his words.

"I was on a Boy Scout trip," he goes on. "We were camping in the woods a day's drive from home. I was so excited, a city kid on my first overnight trip, out in the wild." He shudders. "I don't know how I got separated from the group, but I was alone in the forest for four days before they found me. Everyone thought I was a goner. I can't remember much about it, just . . ." He flexes his hands and looks down at his fingers as if he's surprised to see them still there, attached to his hands. "I don't much like forests."

"So being in this creepy dead forest brought that old memory back," Ana says. "No wonder you panicked, suddenly getting hit with something like that." But even as she's reassuring him, she can't shake the feeling that the trance Todd fell into was more than just some remembered trauma.

Todd makes a noise in his throat, like he's trying to shrug off the incident but not quite succeeding. For one crazy second Ana wants to throw her arms around him, wants to hold him and say everything's going to be okay. Instead she meets his gaze as he turns to face her.

"We're gonna make it," she says, wishing she could say more, wishing she *knew* more. "We're making good time, and once we get to the sea, we'll find out what's going on."

"I guess." Todd walks over to sit next to her on the long, flat stone.

"So much for amnesia, huh?" Ana says. "What's the use of

having no memory if the first thing to come back is all the crap that you actually *want* to be rid of? And at the worst possible time, too."

He frowns at this, and Ana could kick herself for making a bad thing worse. She doesn't know what to say to fix it, but then Todd clears his throat, like he's ready to put all that behind him. "I don't know about you," he says, "but I'm starving."

"Oh, definitely," she says. "Right now, I could eat a giant worm."

Todd looks at her with such a shocked expression that she bursts out laughing, surprised at how easily it bubbles up, how it makes everything else seem insignificant—even if just for this moment. She opens her pack and roots around inside. "Mac-and-cheese? Beef stew? Sweet-and-sour chicken?"

"Yes, yes, and yes."

She grins. "Your call."

"Fine, beef stew."

"You read my mind." She grabs two packets of beef stew, tosses him one, and turns her attention to her own. The instructions are printed on the package, but Ana must have used these before, because the actions are instinctive. She gives the packet three good shakes, then rips the top cleanly off. This unseals the outer heating pack, which she peels back and folds over the bottom half, punching the heating tabs into their slots. She puffs the packet out so it stands on its own. The whole time her hands are going through the motions, there's no thought involved. She grins a little when she realizes this. Another piece of her lost self being reclaimed.

"The famous three-minute readymeal," Todd says with a grin. Ana smiles as she sees those words printed on the wrapper.

Each packet has a biodegradable spork attached to the outside, and before long Ana and Todd are sitting side by side, picking carrots and potatoes and chunks of lean meat out of the silvery wrapper, under a cotton candy sky, with the Dead Forest at their feet.

"Beef stew at the end of the universe," Ana says.

Todd turns to her and his look is a little too serious, as if there's something he might want to say, if he could get it out. Then he sighs and stuffs another bite into his mouth.

"Beef stew appears to agree with you," Ana says, not sure if she should be disappointed by his not sharing whatever was on his mind.

Todd smiles easily. "One hundred percent daily additives!"

She smirks as she sees that he's still quoting from the packaging, and wants to laugh at the incongruity of the situation. The odd moment has passed and they return to eating, but there was something there, something she might recognize if she saw it in another light, something she doesn't really want to think about right now.

Instead, she finishes her meal, turns the packet inside out to start the biodegrading process, then leans back onto her elbows on the stone surface. She throws her arms out flat to either side, feeling the stretch all the way down the muscles of her back.

Her fingers, dangling off the sides of the rock, brush up against a cluster of something small and knobby. She cranes her head over the edge and looks down. A small vine is growing out of a fissure in the rock, and it's heavy with small gray berries.

Curious, she plucks one. It's firm, like a chunky blueberry. She squeezes, and the berry bursts. A trickle of pinkish-purple juice runs down her finger.

"Todd," she says, "do you know what these are?"

He scoots off the rock and crouches down next to her. "Rockberries, sure. Word on the street is they're just about the best berry in the galaxy!"

He laughs out loud, and Ana figures it's as much for the bit of knowledge, trivial as it might seem, as for the fruit itself.

"They grow out of the rock?" Ana asks.

"Sure. They taste good, too." Todd plucks one off the stem and leans toward her. She freezes as his fingers graze her cheek. Her heart pounding in her chest, she parts her lips and he pops the berry in. She bites down, and the tiny fruit fills her mouth with a tart sweetness that is like a bite of blue sunshine. "Oh!" she gasps.

He rubs his fingers together, and his thoughtful look gives her a strange discomfort, a fluttering in her chest that she's quick enough to recognize and smart enough—*Honestly, Ana! Now is not the time for boy thoughts!*—to quash immediately. She leans over the side of the rock and starts harvesting the berries. "I'll beat you to the patch, then," she says.

He grins and shoulders her out of the way. They empty the little vine in minutes, making a mad dash for the last few and then turning to chase the ones that have tumbled onto the grass.

Finally Ana collapses on the ground. The fullness in her belly spreads down to her toes, a warm satisfaction that she wishes she could capture and keep in a bottle.

Todd lies sprawled next to her, his eyes closed. Ana studies him, considering the curve of his jaw, the jut of his cheekbone. There's a twist of thornbush stem twined in his hair and she reaches over to tug it free. He opens his eyes, and his look jolts her. Then a sharp pain in her finger makes her jump. She looks down to see a thorn halfway into the pad of her index finger.

Todd takes her hand in his, pulls off the thorn stem, and tosses it away. As he rubs her finger, she holds his gaze. "I . . ." She stops. What can she say? That she doesn't know what's going on but she thinks she might want to follow it and see where it leads? That when he looks at her with that sleepy half smile, she has a desperate wish to capture this moment and keep it forever?

It's ridiculous enough to even think these things, so she doesn't say anything; she just sits and fills her memory with his face.

Then the peace is shattered by something so unexpected

that Ana can only sit up and goggle in wide-mouthed shock.
Two figures throw long shadows in the high morning sunslight. Two forward-striding, rapidly approaching forms, coming, calling—*yelling!*—with voices that ring out across the
wide clearing.

"Hiya, strangers! Thought you'd never show up! Had time
to miss us yet?"

SEVEN

00:17:31:09

Todd is up and moving so fast that he's halfway across the clearing before Ana has even fully registered what she's hearing. Words! Honest-to-goodness, spoken-out-loud-by-people words!

By the time she scrambles to her feet and starts off after him, Todd is up ahead confronting the two newcomers. There's aggression all over his posture, though they don't seem especially threatening.

Ana slips a hand inside her vest to check for the solidity of the pistol, wishing she'd thought to pull it out earlier to see how it works. Hoping that her muscle memory will do its thing if it comes to that, she strides toward the group.

"Todd?" she calls. "Everything okay over here?"

It's as if someone has pulled the plug on the discussion. Todd's antagonistic stance melts away. The two strangers, a guy and a girl, look up in Ana's direction.

The guy lifts his hands in the air, palms up. "We come in peace," he says, giving her a cocky grin. He's got short, spiky hair and a wiry build and enough attitude to power a rocket. "No wicked thoughts here whatsoever. I'm Chen."

"Ysa," says the girl standing next to him. She's small-boned and pale, with white-blond hair and an easy, graceful manner. Her smile looks strong enough to hold.

Ana realizes two things immediately. One, the newcomers are both around the same age as she and Todd. And two, they are both wearing the same jumpsuit and backpack. She thinks back to the rocket and the two sealed doors she'd assumed were for fuel or storage or whatever she thought when she saw them hours ago.

"You're from the ship, too?" Ana exclaims. "I'm starting to wonder how many of us there are. Every time I turn around it seems like there's another rat running this maze."

Chen smirks. "We're it, baby. Just the four of us, jetting across space on some half-assed mission. Doesn't that just rock your world?"

Ysa nudges him with a grimace, then reaches out her hand. "Ignore him, really. It's good to meet up with you."

"I'm Ana. And the more the better out here, I figure." Ana reaches out her hand to clasp the girl's, though as she does, the gesture feels weird for some reason she can't define. Ysa's hands are milk white, but it's not the contrast between her skin and Ana's own rich tan that gives her pause. It's something more to do with feel. *But . . . what?* Is it a memory trying to break through?

It's not landing, so Ana brushes the thought aside and releases Ysa's hand. Chen nods and extends his for a fist bump.

Ana grins. "You've got to be kidding."

Chen just shifts his pack on his shoulders with a loud laugh. "Come on, fellow stargazers. We have plenty of ground to cover and a tightly budgeted time purse."

Todd nods. "Next destination, the summit at Mount Fahr."

"I'm Chen Wai," Chen says, "and I will be your guide on this planetary expedition. If you turn fully to your left, you will see the awe-inspiring, skyscraping Timor range, home of the only known active volcano in the Cyclid system."

In spite of herself, Ana laughs. Chen takes off at a zesty pace, with Todd following right on his heels. Ana falls into step behind them next to Ysa. The other girl moves confidently across the uneven terrain, but between that and the pack on her shoulders, she seems to be operating at full capacity. Her breath is already coming in quick bursts. Despite this, she looks over at Ana with a friendly smile and a nod. "Doing okay with all of this?" she asks.

Ana smiles back. "I could ask you the same."

"I'm not as puny as I look," Ysa says with a laugh. But she puffs a little to smooth out her breathing. They walk in silence for a few minutes; then Ysa clears her throat. "I wonder, uh . . .

well, Todd told us that both of you guys don't have any personal memories?"

Ana goes suddenly still. *You guys?*

Ysa's got her eyes on the ground in front of her, fully caught up in her own thoughts. "I just can't even imagine it. Can I ask . . . well, what does it feel like? You really don't remember *anything?*"

"Wait," Ana says, grabbing Ysa's arm. "You mean your memory *wasn't* wiped?"

Ysa's eyes widen, like maybe she's worried she said the wrong thing. "No," she says slowly. "Not me or Chen."

Everything around Ana comes into sharp focus. "Then you know what we're doing here! Right? You know what the mission is, why our memories are gone, everything!" She wants to laugh out loud.

Ysa opens her mouth, but at just that moment Ana hears a sound she had hoped to never hear again. It's far away, but she'd know that grinding anywhere.

"Oh, no," Ana says, exhilaration falling away from her in one great swoop.

All four of them stop. Chen says hoarsely, "What the hell is making that sound?"

"The worm," Todd says. He turns to Ana, brows drawn sharply together. "Could it be following us?"

"What are you two talking about?" Ysa asks, panic in her voice. "What worm? There's no animal life on Paradox— definitely nothing that could make a noise like *that!*"

69

"It sounds like fire," Chen whispers. "Like licking tongues of flame. And voices . . ."

It sounds nothing of the sort, of course. As it has from the first, the sound of the worm's approach is a harsh metallic grinding. And it's getting louder by the second, even though the creature isn't yet visible. Ana takes a few steps back down the slope, testing the worm-killing passion she'd felt earlier. It's still there, and she can't help thinking how much better their odds would be now that there are four of them.

"What do we do?" Ysa wails. "I don't understand what's going on!"

On the other hand, maybe not so much better.

"It's some kind of huge creature, looks almost like a worm—if a worm were the size of a train," she tells Ysa. "We ran into it back at the crater. I just don't understand how it's found us again."

"It can't have come through the forest," Todd says. "We'd have seen trees shaking or falling or something. It must have gone around."

"Around? And it was at the crater with you?" Chen echoes. His lightness sounds forced as he says, "Then we'd be dealing with Superworm. Moving at the speed of light!"

Ana thinks of the way the worm was attacking the rock face back at the crater. "Could it have gone underground?"

"I don't want to hear anymore," says Ysa. "Let's just get moving."

"We'd better find some shelter," Todd says.

Chen lets out a whoop, and Ana turns to look at him, startled. "Shelter!" he says. "Where better than inside the mountain? Come on, I know just the place."

"You're thinking of the caves," Ysa says, relief breaking over her face. She pushes past Chen and tackles the incline. Todd and Chen follow, and Ana brings up the rear. Getting out of the worm's reach is obviously the right choice, but still she can't quite dismiss the fight fuel that's lacing the pit of her stomach.

The grinding sound gets suddenly louder, and Ana glances back over her shoulder. In the meadow where she and Todd first stopped to rest, the worm bursts into view from behind a gentle slope, like maybe it really did rise up from under the ground. Mud-pink and monstrous even from this distance, its body is made up of overlapping plates that grind against each other, and its head has two cavernous eyeholes and a slash of a mouth that splits it neatly down the middle. As she watches, that mouth opens in a silent grimace, showing a tunnel of teeth—three, four, six razor-sharp rows.

Realizing she's come to a complete standstill, Ana turns and looks for the others, expecting to have been left behind. Instead, all three are standing equally motionless near her, mouths agape.

"Hey," she says. When there's no change, no response at all to her call, she yells again, "HEY!"

Like a rubber band snapping, the others come out of their stupor. It's obviously an effort, but Ysa turns away from the worm and back to the slope, with the rest following close behind. Chen leapfrogs over a boulder, gesturing as he mutters to Ysa beside him. Ysa is nodding frantically as her breath comes in loud puffs. Only Todd pulls off to the side for a moment, fumbling with his circlet as if he's trying to check something on it.

"Come on," Ana says. The grinding is growing louder by the second.

He nods and waves her on. He might feel the need to double-check the path, but with the worm this close, she's willing to chance that Chen knows where he's going. Still . . .

"This cave," Ana calls up between breaths. "Is it much farther?"

"Nah," Chen yells back over the worm's noise. "Not far at all. See up there?"

Ana scans the slope ahead and almost doesn't see the opening, nestled as it is in a cluster of undergrowth and rugged-looking boulders. It's small, too, not more than a couple feet across.

"That's perfect!" She's panting around every word, but doesn't slow her pace. "There's no way the worm will be able to get in after us."

"A-plus for the obvious, Anagram," Chen crows, and Ana would have thrown him a dirty look if she could have spared the time and energy. She does look back for Todd and he's moving again, only a few paces back.

Chen's version of *not far* takes them nearly ten minutes of flat-out climbing, with the worm gaining at an alarming rate. By the time Ysa yells and tears through the dark, shadowed entrance, Chen is just a few strides behind her, Todd is panting right beside Ana, and the worm's breath is a hot wind at their backs.

The ground is shaking like an earthquake, and all around them rocks tremble loose and careen down the hill.

"Come on!" Chen yells back as he runs. "Hurry it up!"

Ignoring the tearing in her side, Ana puts on a burst of speed and shoots ahead of Todd. Ysa has vanished inside the cave. Chen reaches the entrance next. He darts through, but skids to a stop right in the entrance, spinning around and looking back toward Ana and Todd, chest heaving with exertion.

Then his mouth drops open and his eyes go wide. "No!" he yells.

Ana's legs are shaking so hard it's all she can do to control them. She shoots through the opening like a sprung arrow, then collapses against the wall, panting, trying to regain her breath.

"Todd!" she hears Chen yell. "Get up, man!"

She can barely hear Chen over the worm's cacophony, but the horror in his voice is unmistakable. A jolt of adrenaline courses through her as she pushes herself up from the wall and darts over to the cave's mouth. Chen is leaning out, staring back behind them at . . .

Todd.

He's sprawled on the ground just outside the cave, his

backpack askew. He seems to have fallen, but he's not getting up. *Why isn't he getting up?*

The worm is right behind him, and Ana could swear she sees hunger and blood and death roiling in its bottomless eyes. It grinds slowly over the rocky ground, almost as if savoring this final approach.

"Todd!" Chen screams again, and Todd turns back in their direction. An uncertain look crosses his face and he climbs slowly to his feet. But then he half turns again and glances back at the worm.

A spasm of fear crosses his face. He freezes.

Chen is still yelling, and Ana joins him, but it's no use. Nothing seems to be able to break through the worm's din this time to reach Todd. He's just standing there motionless, staring up at the worm.

Suddenly Ana can't stand it. *I've got to do something!*

She charges out of the cave and crashes straight into Todd. The impact sends him careening into the shrubbery off to the side, out of the worm's path. Ana dives after him, but thrown off balance by the shift in weight, she skids and topples to the ground herself. Now she's the one in front of the worm, gasping at the sudden tearing pain in her shoulder.

The worm stretches its jaws wide.

She thought its breath would smell like death, but it doesn't. It smells like chamomile, like comfort, like peace. Is this what Todd felt a few seconds ago? Is this what kept him frozen in place?

Fighting the fog in her mind and the horrible din in her ears, Ana drags herself off to the side, out of the worm's direct path, but there's little point. All the monster has to do is turn its head, angle its gaping mouth in her direction, and she will be finished.

Ana closes her eyes and waits as the ground around her ripples and rolls.

And then . . .

Nothing happens.

She opens her eyes and sees the giant scaly body of the worm grinding on past her, continuing toward the cave entrance.

What?

There's a yank on her pack and she is propelled backward into the bushes.

"You're insane, you know that?" Todd hisses in her ear, gripping her shoulders, and it doesn't even matter that Ana wants to scream in pain as he jostles her injury, because she's alive—*alive!* She's safe. Todd's safe. And inside the cave, Ysa and Chen are going to be all right, too.

"Come on," Todd says. "Let's get moving before that thing wises up and comes to sniff us out."

"Get moving where?"

"There's another cave we can get to; the opening's just a little higher up."

Todd grabs her hand and together they push through the undergrowth, skirting around to the rear of the worm's massive body, the roars filling the space behind them. The pressure of Todd's grip fills Ana with a heady sort of strength.

With one hand in Todd's, she thinks, *I might be able to do anything on this crazy planet. Survive the worm and live to fight another day and everything.*

The thought is ridiculous enough to bring a blush to her cheeks.

But she doesn't let go of his hand.

Together they double back and start up the slope again while below them the worm pounds its great head against the mountain face over and over and over.

Long minutes later, with the worm's noise still grinding around them, they arrive at a clearing. Right at its heart is a tiny opening, so small it looks like the burrow of a woodland animal.

"We'll have to push our packs in front of us," Todd says.

Ana looks doubtfully at the opening. "You think the passage opens up inside?"

"Definitely," Todd says. He gestures toward the slope. "Look at the size of this mountain. How could it not?"

He has a point, and she doesn't have a better idea. Sheer luck might have saved her last time, or maybe the worm's lack of peripheral vision, but she's not going to push it by staying out in the open while that thing is anywhere nearby.

Suddenly the adrenaline that's been churning through her seems to disappear all at once and her knees buckle. "What happened back there?"

Todd grabs her arm to steady her. "You saved my life, that's what happened."

Ana shakes her head, but somehow her eyes are full of tears. She leans toward Todd, drops her head on his shoulder, and cries. Only for a few seconds, then she sniffs and rubs her nose. "Sorry," she mutters.

"Hey," says Todd, "you can muddy up my jumpsuit any-time, Ana. You own me."

She looks into his eyes and is surprised again at how blue they are, sketched in full color against the dull undergrowth. The worm's rage echoes off the rocks, yet it could be in an-other world altogether.

Ana opens her mouth to speak, but Todd breaks her gaze and looks down. "We'd better get into that cave."

Ana swallows. "Yeah," she says. "Anyway, we're even. You saved me last time. It's only fair."

Todd gives her a half grin. "I did, didn't I?" He looks at her shoulder. "How's your arm holding up?"

"Fine." There's some pain when she moves, but it's nothing she can't manage. The important thing right now is getting out of the worm's reach.

With a nod, Todd drops his pack and pushes it into the opening, then shimmies through after it. Ana feels as if she shouldn't be staring quite so obviously at the way the fabric of Todd's jumpsuit moves over his thighs and the backs of his legs.

But she doesn't look away.

Then it's her turn. Pushing her pack before her, she crawls into the cave. The sound of rocks crumbling in the distance, the worm continuing its assault on the mountain, fades behind her. Beyond the opening the cave widens, just as Todd predicted. Not much light makes it through the small entrance, and Ana runs her hands along the nearby wall for support as she climbs to her feet.

"Todd?"

"Shhhhh."

"Where are you? I can't—"

"Here," he says, and she feels his hand grip her arm.

Ana gropes around for her pack and shoulders it. With one hand holding Todd's and the other still trailing the cave wall, she follows Todd deeper and deeper into the darkness. Finally, they come to a stop. Ana drops her backpack and collapses against the wall.

She glances at her circlet and its glowing numbers. Barely sixteen hours left, and they have a whole mountain to cross— and who knows what after that.

"How long can we afford to stay in here, do you think?" she asks.

"I'll check in a half hour or so," Todd says out of the darkness. "See whether the worm's gone, then find the others."

Ana yawns. She can't help it. She's been pushing for hours, and that last run squeezed out her final drops of energy. She thinks she could happily sit here in the darkness, holding Todd's hand, for the rest of her life.

Wait . . . holding Todd's hand? *Still?*

Cheeks flaming, she slides her fingers out of his.

She hears Todd settling on the ground next to her and keeps expecting her eyes to adjust to the dark, thinks she'll start seeing the faint shapes and outlines of the things around her. But there's nothing. Not even the faint glow from her circlet can penetrate the gloom. It's like being part of the night sky. She could easily bring up the map and get some light that way, but there doesn't seem to be any point. It's warm in here, too.

Weariness sweeps over her in a rush and she's sleepy—so sleepy—

"Take this." Todd's whisper is gentle and low. "You should eat something."

"What?" she mumbles. "Not . . ." He's sliding something at her, but she can't think about that right now. She feels him press a package into one of her jumpsuit pockets. She's in a hammock, hung between two stars. She's lying on a comet. She is the night sky.

"Hope the others got away safely, that they aren't—" A yawn swallows the rest of her words.

Funny how this darkness works. In the silence she can hear Todd's face wrinkle into a smile. She smiles in return and wonders if he can hear her, too.

"I'm sure they're fine."

How did she ever think it was dark in here? She can't see the moon, but the stars are more than bright enough. The nearest one is just a leap away. If she stands just so—she leans her foot way back, and *jumps.*

She looks around her. What she's landed on isn't a star at all; it's a planet, a small red planet with a wide yellow ring around it. No . . . not a ring but a worm, circling the planet, with gnashing, slavering jaws. Then her feet are disappearing into the ground and the stars overhead are getting closer and she's being swallowed up by light.

And then even that is gone.

EIGHT

00:13:38:31

Ana opens her eyes. She closes them. She opens them again.

For a second panic courses through her. She reaches her hands out to either side, half expecting to feel the plush velvet cushions of her rocket. It couldn't be—

It isn't.

Her left hand smacks into a stone wall and she gasps. Where is she? Then it all comes back.

"Todd!" she says. The word echoes around her, a hollow, empty sound. "Todd?"

Ana fumbles for her right wrist and activates her circlet. The rocky room—a small alcove, tucked just off a wider chamber—fills with the map's glow. Blinking, she looks at the countdown.

She's been sleeping for over two hours!

She staggers to her feet, her neck stiff and her shoulder on fire. "Todd!" she calls.

Todd . . . Todd . . . Todd . . .

The echo boomerangs around the hollow chamber.

Okay, think. Ana tries to quell the panic surging in her. *He's probably just gone to check on the others, to see if the worm is gone. He'll be back in a few minutes. But . . . two hours?*

And why would he go by himself, without waking her?

Ana stumbles out into the main chamber, where a corridor winds out of sight in both directions. Which way did they come in?

To her right, the trail curves gently downward, while to the left it takes a sharp turn up. This is a mountain cave, going in and up the mountain, so it seems clear that going down will lead back to the exit. Ana heaves the pack onto her back, with a wince of pain for her still-aching shoulder. She aims the map ahead and turns down the gently sloping path.

The way narrows pretty quickly and the ceiling grows steadily lower. She follows the winding corridor until finally she sees a circle of daylight near the floor—the entrance! She switches off the map and, pushing her pack before her, emerges, blinking, into the sunlight of the woodsy copse. The air is fresh and cool compared to the dank mustiness inside the cave and, best of all, there is absolutely no worm noise.

Of course, Todd is nowhere in sight.

It's not as if she expected him to be hovering outside the

cave, waiting for her, but she still can't help feeling left behind. Unexpectedly there's a flash in her mind: the image of an open grave with a cascade of dirt pouring down onto a polished wooden casket. A quaking emptiness and tangible sense of isolation punches her in the gut.

What was that? A reclaimed memory, obviously, or some fragment of one. She considers suddenly the benefit there might be in the complete loss of one's past. Just a sliver of that scene was almost enough to send her to her knees. What would it feel like to carry the weight of the whole experience?

With effort, Ana pulls herself back to the present and sets off for the first cave opening. As she navigates the slope, she remembers the food packets Todd had pressed on her back in the cave. She finds them in one of her front pockets, suddenly ravenous. In short order she tosses down three water capsules, a packet of dried fruit, and two tabs of desiccated bran muffins. A full-sized energy bar rounds off the meal.

The silence holds as she makes her way down the slope. Once she clears the trees in front of the first cave, though, her heart sinks.

This is no longer an entryway: it's a burial site. The worm is gone, but it's taken half the mountain face with it. All that's left is a rockslide of rubble, boulders bigger than she is heaped in a pile twenty or thirty feet high.

No one is getting out of this cave.

Something inside Ana shrivels to a tiny point of focused light. In desperation she touches her circlet, pulls up the map, and holds it out in front of her. The blinking red-dotted line is still there, steady as ever.

What now? Todd came into her life out of nowhere, and Ysa and Chen were around for only a few minutes before the worm appeared. What scares her, what truly terrifies her, is how much she suddenly feels like she needs them in order to go on. For a moment she actually considers just pitching her tent and waiting here for Todd to find her. Waiting until they can move forward together, as a team, conducting their joint mystery-mission.

And that thought, that terrible, desperate need, is enough to galvanize her to action. In less time than it takes her to formulate the thought, Ana has decided. Nothing has changed since she first set foot on Paradox. She has the map; she knows the final destination.

She can't wait around for anyone. She doesn't need anyone else. She can't afford to.

She's going on alone.

First Wave of Space Colonists Departs for Paradox

National News Network

To much fanfare, the first expedition of scientist-explorers heading for the planet Cyclid-Bf, popularly known as Paradox, departed Monday from the Austin Space Launch Facility. The launch follows nearly two decades of coordinated research, preparation, and planning across four continents.

The group of eight colonists that comprises the first Paradox expedition—or APEX1—includes leading botanists, geologists, and astrobiologists specializing in space-related applications. "We can't wait to see what's out there," said Savitech lead geologist James Ortez. "This is hands down the biggest astronomical opportunity of the century."

Colonists will make the trip in a state of partially suspended animation, due to spatial confines of the rocket necessary to fit the massive neo-Alc warp drives. Major funding and sponsorship have been provided by Savitech, and streaming communications will be handled by ParSpace's breakthrough real-time signal-dispersion technology. "We've run through the full spectrum of tests with ParSpace technicians," said Ortez. "There shouldn't be more than a half-hour lag time on either end, no matter how far out we are."

With an estimated 3.5-month travel time, the APEX1 rocket is expected to reach Paradox by the end of January.

NINE

00:12:59:48

No sooner has she made this decision than Ana is on her way. She lines up the map, charts the quickest way up the mountain, then sets off at a brisk pace. It seems like just a few minutes ago that she and Todd were tearing along this same route, the worm's crushing din behind them, and Ana again suppresses a pang over her missing companions.

Once she leaves the lowlands behind, the mountainside is rocky and almost completely bare of plant life. There's some hardy scrub and a few spindly skeleton plants that might have come straight from the Dead Forest. But that's it.

Over everything rises the permeating smell of sulfur. It's so strong, in fact, that less than half an hour into her climb, Ana's eyes start watering. She leans into the slope, shifts her backpack so it's centered between her shoulders—wincing as she grinds her still-painful shoulder—pops another water capsule, and climbs on. There's no trail, no path, no obvious way up. After skidding down several mini rock slides, she pulls up her map and zooms in and out, looking for an easier course of ascent. Then she sees it: a stream winds all the way up the mountain, leading right to the peak. She'll have to go a little out of her way at first, but then she can follow it straight to the top.

The farther she climbs, the better Ana's shoulder feels. She'd thought the constant motion would worsen the pain, but the opposite seems true. It's as if she's jarring things back into place. Unless she pokes the spot with her fingers, the pain is just a dull twinge. Her forehead, too, is almost as good as new; when she touches it, she can hardly tell where the peri ends and her own skin begins. There's just the smallest raised scar where her skin was hanging open a few hours ago.

She glances at her circlet. Almost two hours have passed since she woke up alone in the cave. She can't help wondering whether Todd and Ysa and Chen are all right.

She stops to catch her breath and wipe some of the sweat from her forehead. And then—just up ahead, she sees a dark glint in the pale sunlight. The stream! Ana gets moving again with renewed energy. But when she reaches the bank, a cloud of fumes sweeps over her and she has to cover her mouth and nose against the smell.

"That's not water at all," she whispers. "It's—"

It's a river of lava, issuing from the summit of the volcano and coursing down the slope in a wide, lazy flow. It's over six feet across and moves soundlessly, coal black with a tinge of red and little curlicues of steam rising from it. Heat waves ripple on the surface.

Unpleasant as it may be, it's a surefire ticket to the top of the slope. Holding her breath in ten- to fifteen-second intervals, she turns and starts walking along the bank.

Hold. Count, gulp, hold.

And like this the time slips away.

She's walking some, climbing more, sometimes resorting to grabbing at rocks and lugging herself up steep inclines. In these places, the lava pours down from the sheer rock face in a macabre cascade. It flows so slowly that it almost appears static, each fold and ripple like the photographic negative of a waterfall. It's eerie and magical and horrible all at once.

Ana's so transfixed by the stream that she nearly misses the sparkle. But then she looks up, and—*could it be?* Yes, there it is, just up ahead . . . a twisting strand of glinting light.

It all comes back in a rush: the irresistible pull, the quick slip into another world, the fullness of being even for just a few minutes someone who knows herself inside and out. Another strand means another memory, hers for the keeping.

The craving is like a dull ache in her core, shocking her with how quickly it takes over every aspect of her awareness.

Ana shrugs off her backpack, lets it fall behind her, and runs.

A gust of wind catches the memory strand as Ana approaches, tugging it just out of reach. She stretches her arms above her head. She *has* to catch that strand. *Has to has to has to.*

In a pocket of stillness the glittering thread drops down toward her. It glides over her hands, coating her in its mirror-light spray . . . and she is gone.

"—have to go! He's dead, damn it, don't you understand?" I feel myself crumple inside. How did everything fall apart so quickly? Wasn't it just hours ago that I was thinking about that playoff game? When did everything go so hellishly wrong?

Jackson's yelling now, his voice rough. I don't want to hear what he says, and I pull the receiver away from my ear. I don't want to hear that Brian's as good as dead now that he's infected and that my being there won't bring him back, that I'll just get sick too if I go back home, that my place is here in the lab. Where there's still a chance.

I slam the phone back onto the receiver and jump up. I've got to get out of here. I'm halfway across the office before I even finish forming the thought. But then Pat's in front of me, head sticking out of his cube, eyebrows creased in worry.

"Hey," he says. "I heard about Brian. I'm so sorry."

I'm crying so hard I trip over that stupid fold in the carpet that nobody ever bothers to fix, and I crumple to the floor. What does it matter? What does anything matter? Right in front of me there's a paper stuck to the wall, a paper I taped up less than twenty-four hours ago, this week's company lunch sign-up. The day after tomorrow. Will anyone still be alive to make that pizza order?

"We're going to make it through this," Pat says, though I can hardly hear him above my sobbing. "You'll see—things will get better. What about the new theory?"

"The whole world," I snap. "The whole world's gone to hell. What does our research matter if everyone's dead? So there's some kind of core inter-linked entity, so it's theoretically reversible—so what? We still don't know how to stop it in the first place, how to keep away the—"

I won't say it. I won't say the word. If I don't say it, maybe it's not real.

I struggle to my feet. Jackson was right. There's nothing for me to go home to, not anymore. Not that things are any better here, of course—the place is all but deserted, just the empty cubicles and the screened-in trial area.

Pat has ducked back down behind his divider. I sigh as I make my way back to my own cube. I know he didn't deserve my outburst, but all I want to do is feel sorry for myself. It's all I can manage right now.

My wedding ring catches my eye again. And, oh! Brian! And I want to cry all over again for everything we've lost, everything I and we and this whole damn world will never have.

I drop to my seat just as the phone begins to ring. "Yeah?"

"Bailey." It's Jackson again, and his voice sounds worse than it did just minutes ago. "Bailey—"

And then he coughs, loud and long. A chill runs through me.

"Jackson? What are you—"

Ana comes back to herself with a gasp. She's facedown on the ground, just like the last time she emerged from the memory strand, but now her hand is hanging over the edge of the lava stream. She yanks it back and slowly sits up. She is dripping with sweat and her heart is racing. This was nothing like the first memory; this was some kind of nightmare. Who is, or was, this Bailey? Was everyone in her world sick? Ana wonders how she can feel so much sympathy for someone she's never met, someone who's probably long since dead, who—*let's be honest here*—very possibly doesn't even exist.

Hauling herself to her feet, Ana hikes down the hill to get her backpack. She pulls it up with muscles that are tight and stiff and shoulders that scream at resuming their burden. She grits her teeth against the pain and thinks of Bailey. Nothing Ana is feeling now comes close to the gut-wrenching pain she felt during those brief moments living in Bailey's head.

She turns to face the mountain, telling herself the tears on her cheeks are just a reaction to the thick, noxious fumes. And then a sound reaches her on the sulfuric breeze, ringing faintly up the slope.

It's useless, it's nothing, it's one more thing she really doesn't need, but . . . somehow it's also the very thing she most wants.

"Ana!" She can hear the call clearly now. "Is that you? Wait up already!"

TEN

00:10:03:07

Todd is climbing up the slope toward her at a double-quick pace, with Ysa and Chen not far behind.

"What"—Todd puffs as he gets closer—"on Earth"—puff—"okay, *off* Earth"—puff—"but *what* the hell do you think you're doing? Where did you go? I got back . . ."

Inwardly, Ana grins. She can't help it. She feels ridiculous and sheepish, but oh, to be missed! Maybe worried about, even. There's nothing like it.

Still, she forces herself to arch a cool eyebrow. "You vanished," she said. "How was I supposed to know when you were coming back? *If* you were coming back? It's not like we even know each other all that well."

He winces. "Okay, I guess. But really? We're traveling companions. You should know that much."

Despite herself, something inside Ana relaxes. She *is* glad to be back with the others, in spite of all her power-of-one assertions. But the situation also grates a little. It's as if it's teasing out a dependency she thought she'd gotten away from but that has now caught up with her—something she wants but fears, maybe, or wants but doesn't quite trust.

"I suppose," she concedes. "So where *did* you go?"

He tips his head toward Ysa and Chen, who are finally catching up. "We talked about this, remember? I went for the others."

"Yeah, but *two* hours?"

"Anagram!" Chen whoops. Unlike the other two, he doesn't seem to be breaking a sweat, though he's not hurrying, either. "You crazy piece of space rocket! Led us on quite a chase, my gal. But ain't that just what you do?"

Ysa looks sharply at Chen, and suddenly Ana remembers her aborted conversation with Ysa, back when the worm showed up. Ana and Todd had this surgical amnesia procedure, but Ysa and Chen didn't. They still have their memories intact. And they all came in the same rocket. Of course!

"We knew each other," she says to Chen. "Didn't we? Before my memory got the axe, I mean."

Chen opens his mouth and closes it, his goofiness suddenly gone. He takes a step backward.

Ana looks back and forth between Ysa and Chen. "What's going on? Did I say something wrong?"

Ysa steps forward and puts a hand on Ana's arm. "Look," she says gently.

Ana shakes her off. "This is not a tough question! Did. We. Know each other?"

Chen looks Ana in the eye. "Yes," he says. "Okay? We knew you. Know you. But—"

"But we can't talk about it," Ysa interrupts.

"What?" Ana says. "You can't talk about *what*?"

"Anything to do with the, er, past. Yours or ours." Ysa's face is red and she looks miserable. Chen is studying the ground with great concentration.

Ana can't decide whether to be enraged or utterly confused. "I just don't understand what the big deal is. Todd's and my memories are gone, and we want to know why. We want to know what we're here for. What is the real purpose of this mission? That's really too much to ask?"

"It's really not," Chen says. "It's not too much at all. If you ask me, this whole thing totally sucks." But he doesn't volunteer anything further, and finally Ysa continues.

"We're not allowed to talk about it. Any of those things you said—what and who and why and all that. Really. It's part of the mission, and it's important. *Really* important. We can't say anything more about it than that, and even that much"— she shoots a glower at Chen—"is more than we should have said."

"Are you kidding me?"

"Trust me," Ysa says. "It's all going to make sense. We just have to get to the end."

Todd cuts in. "The colony, zero hour, end of the countdown. Right?"

"Zero hour," Chen agrees, but his voice sounds strained. "When everything becomes clear. Now can we get back to the forced march, people?"

A red haze pulses on the edge of Ana's vision. For a few moments she doesn't trust herself to speak. But the confusion and fear she can see on Chen's and Ysa's faces make it clear how serious they are. *What the hell is going on?*

"Fine," she says, forcing herself to take slow, measured breaths. "Let's get going." She throws a glance at Todd to see his reaction to this whole debacle, but his back is turned and he's already climbing.

She looks at her circlet. Ten hours to go. Is she really supposed to wait until then? *Well, there's more than one way to season the soup,* she thinks, and the expression jars her, like something distantly misremembered, but she knows what she's taking from it right now.

There's knowledge to be had, things that she desperately wants to—*has to*—know. But Ana knows how to be patient. She can work different ways toward a goal. She can set a course and come around at it from the sides, can work toward an end result without letting on, without making it obvious—and without ever giving up.

She'll bide her time. But she *will* get to the bottom of this.

With that thought resolved to her satisfaction, Ana looks up and down the slope and is surprised both by how far she has come and by the distance yet to scale. They're maybe halfway up the mountain, and it looks like the most challenging portion of the climb is still to come.

"It just gets better from here," Chen croons, doing a little tap dance. "Come on, mountain baby, do your worst!"

With a groan Ana rotates her sore shoulder, grateful that the pain is staying manageable, then tackles the slope. "How did you guys get out, anyway?" she says after a few minutes. Safe topics. Baby steps. "That cave was completely blocked off."

"The two caves are connected," Todd calls from up ahead. "I got them out the way you and I got in."

"It's a warren in there," Ysa says, panting slightly.

"You got to them from *inside* the caves?" Ana can't believe it. "But how did you guys find your way around?"

"Sheer genius," Chen says, tapping the side of his forehead.

Todd flashes a grin over his shoulder. "Ignore him. As you noted, it took a while. What matters is, we're all out safely, and back together."

Mountain climbing in a group, Ana quickly discovers, is vastly more entertaining than doing so alone. Even her own brooding funk grows lighter the farther they go. Chen moves easily into the lead, keeping up a rolling prattle all the while, often stopping to wait for the rest of them to catch up. Ana's not sure if he's being inclusive by not going too far ahead, or if he just doesn't want to lose the laugh track to his ongoing comedy routine.

They're covering ground at a good pace, still loosely following the lava stream toward the summit. Chen seems to take his position as guide very seriously, sometimes leading them off to the side on unlikely looking detours that always end up at easier climbing spots. He's obviously done his research on this place.

As Ana stops to catch her breath, Chen does a flying leap onto a boulder just ahead and teeters a little on the apex.

"Meet your master!" he bellows to the ground below. "At my feet, minions!"

And so the time goes by—if not flying, not exactly crawling, either. The slope grows steeper the higher they climb, until it takes Ana's full energy and concentration just to keep moving. Her forearms ache, and there's a jagged scratch down the back of her right hand where she caught it on a thorny bush. Inside her suit, her arms feel damp and itchy.

Then she tilts her head and has to bite back a gasp as she realizes how near they are to the top of the mountain. *A hard climb up, sure, but so deliciously near!*

There's a low, mournful sound in the distance, and for one second a cold hand grips Ana's chest. *Could it be?* But no, it's just the wind wailing through the barren mountain scrub.

She catches Todd's eye and knows they are thinking the same thought, fearing the same fear. And she realizes that she is assuming the worm will be back. It has stalked their moves so far—why should it be any different up ahead?

"Our final destination," Ana calls out to the others. "Will there be some kind of worm protection there, you think?"

Todd opens his mouth, then grimaces and shakes his head. "I sure hope so."

"Well, there'd have to be, right?" she says. "It can't be just us the worm is after. No wonder there's no sign of animal life around this place! There must be some sort of shelter for people to have survived at all."

"Survived?" Chen calls over his shoulder, with more venom than she's ever heard from him. "Who said anything about people surviving?"

Ana gapes. "What are you talking about?"

She sees a blur of motion out of the corner of her eye as Ysa pushes past her on the trail and tackles Chen.

"Hey!" he yelps. There's some giggling and some raucous laughter, and Chen topples backpack-first onto the uneven ground and ends up lying like a flipped beetle, waving his hands and feet in the air.

Ana is not impressed. In the chaos she never loses sight of the question, just waits patiently until everything dies down and the two pull each other back up. They take a few steps, then turn back, and she's standing there—*yes, theatrically, I fully realize this*—with her hands on her hips.

"Are you telling me there is *no one* at the colony?" she says slowly.

Ysa glowers at Chen. But when she turns back to Ana, Ana is surprised to see the sunslight glint off a tear track winding down her cheek. "They died," Ysa says softly. "All of them. They're gone."

"Well, not *all* of them," Chen amends. "There's—"

Ysa brushes a hand across her face and shakes her head at

Chen. She fixes Ana with her gaze. "And we really, really can't talk about it. It's like I said before. You'll find out about it all eventually, and believe me—that'll be too soon. But just give it a little longer, okay? Can we leave it for now?"

It's just about too much to take. "No!" Ana explodes. "We *can't* leave it. We're heading to some colony, that's the whole goal of this . . . this mission, or whatever the hell it is. You said that's where we're going to finally be told what's going on. Okay, fine. But now you tell me that there are also *no people there?* Or just a few people, but a bunch of them have died? Or whatever the hell you mean. What is going on here?"

She looks to Todd for support and is surprised to see him shaking his head. "Let's just get where we're going," he says. "There'll be more than enough time to talk it through then. Okay?" He reaches a hand toward her and it's all she can do not to slug him right across his cowardly, nonconfrontational face.

Instead, she launches herself at the mountain, scrambling faster than before, tearing new scratches on her hands and pushing against the stitch growing in her side. She throws her whole soul into the mountain and lets it burrow under her skin, losing herself in the strain of her muscles and the yank in her side that tells her she's doing too much too fast and the wrench of her shoulder as she grits her teeth against the pain.

She knows she can't keep it up, but she just wants some

distance. The others don't call out to her—whether they're conferring among themselves or just giving her space, she has no idea. She only knows she's so angry she can hardly see straight. At Ysa, at Chen—and at Todd most of all, just for being okay with this ridiculous state of affairs when he should be siding with her and backing her up.

She can't keep up this pace forever, though, and after twenty minutes of breakneck climbing, she knows she needs to take it down a notch. She pulls herself onto an overhang that juts out of the rock face, drops her backpack, and collapses onto the warm stone. She pops a few water capsules and rips open a blackberry-nut bar with her teeth, then finally allows herself to look back at the slope face she's just scaled.

It's a spectacular panorama.

The slope rolls below her in an endless wash of rock and dead scrub. The lava stream twists and winds to her left, following the easiest track downhill. She can even see the far-off blanket that is the Dead Forest, though the trees look like scratchy black bristles from this distance.

Todd and the others aren't as far behind as she had expected, though she's gratified to see them, even Chen, red-faced and sweating. Ysa trails the group, looking like the walking dead, and Ana feels a twinge of sympathy that she quashes as quickly as it comes.

A cool wind blows from the east, chilling the sweat that's pooled in Ana's collar. The exertion and the heat rolling off the volcano's slope—not to mention the baking rays of the rapidly rising sun, Torus, which has now halved its distance to its twin—have flushed her cheeks and made her wish she could strip down to her underwear. Finally she feels restored enough to sit up, and she turns around to face the rest of the slope. She gasps.

The summit is so close—it's *right there!* She feels as if she could stretch out one arm and touch it with the tips of her fingers. It can't be more than a ten- or fifteen-minute climb away.

She rubs the energy bar wrapper briskly between her hands until it biodegrades into a fine powder. Then she throws on her backpack and turns to restart her climb.

"Wait," comes a croak from behind her. Ana glances back to see Todd, breathless and waving a strip of white tissue like a flag. His look is pleading, and something inside her gives a quick, sharp pulse. She suddenly thinks back to that moment in the scrub, the clasp of his hand in hers as they fled the worm—and her iron grip on her fury wobbles.

"Please, just wait a second," he says.

"Yeah," calls Chen beside him. "You can't summit on your own. We're a team, even if some of us are psycho!"

In spite of herself, Ana half smiles. *Could I have been overreacting back there?* She considers. Suddenly she's a little ashamed at having made such a big deal out of the situation. There are nine hours to go; is that really so long to wait for answers? If the others think it's that important, does she really need to force the issue? Not to mention storming off like a toddler in a temper tantrum.

She hates to admit it, but maybe Todd had the right idea after all.

With a resigned smile she lifts a hand in agreement. "Get your butts up here, then, because this mountain climber has a goal to reach."

And the sooner she gets there, the better.

ELEVEN

00:09:00:57

Now that she's made peace with the situation, Ana throws herself mindlessly into the rest of the trek. They clear the last bluff, and from there it's an easy climb to the summit.

She marvels at all the Earth-like elements on this planet. Is that why it was chosen for exploration? How long did it take scientists to find Paradox, among the millions of planets in the galaxy? How far away from Earth are they?

She scrambles up alongside Todd, who seems to have located the easiest path to the top.

"Hey," she says. "So tell me about the volcano."

"Mount Fahr," Todd says. He stumbles a little, catches himself with both hands, but keeps moving. "It blew its top thousands of years ago, if I'm not mistaken. The plant life has come back in some areas, but not in others."

Ana whistles. That explains a lot about the vegetation all along the mountain. And even . . . "The Dead Forest!" she says. "No wonder it's all ashy and, um, *dead*." She frowns. "Do you suppose there used to be life on this planet? Real animal life, I mean, more than just the worm?"

"Kaboom!" Chen crows from behind them, apparently still in the volcanic eruption part of the conversation.

"Who knows," says Ysa. "The planet scans were zip on any current life, that's for sure. And virtually no signs were found of any past animal life, either."

"Except the worm," Ana muses, "which isn't supposed to be here anymore, but somehow it is."

Ysa lifts her head quickly and locks eyes with Chen, who frowns. Ana rolls her eyes. More secret stuff, no doubt.

But now their climb is over. First Todd, then Ana, with Chen and Ysa just behind, take their last scrambling steps up and over.

They stand at the very top of Mount Fahr.

The peak is wide and flat—it must go a quarter mile all the way around—and a big gap is hollowed out of the nearest edge, like the first lopsided scoop dug into a tub of ice cream. They all drop their packs in an unspoken agreement to take a few minutes' break. Ana follows the lava flow across the summit to the edge of the crater. Here the rocky surface is cracked and jagged, the slate-gray stone dark and scorched.

This is where the lava stream begins its down-slope journey, but other molten puddles burble and dance around the edge, little spills and trickles of hot melted rock that don't go anywhere in particular.

Ana steps cautiously around the pools and peers into the gaping heart of the mountain. There's not much to see, just smoke and steam. The same horrible stench they've been smelling all the way up the mountain is so strong here it's almost like a physical shove.

And then—"Boo!" There *is* a hand at her back, but it's not shoving her, it's grabbing her to keep her from toppling over the edge of the crater.

"Steady," Chen says. "I've gotcha. Just a friendly jab between travelers."

Ana spins around and socks him in the jaw. It's not much of a punch, but he reels theatrically backward. Ana groans at the pain that ripples across her knuckles. "Don't—ever—do that to me," she growls. "Not anywhere, but definitely not here. Are you an idiot?"

To her surprise, Todd is chuckling and Ysa is laughing out loud. They're sprawled out next to their packs on the flat ground that's set back from the lava pools. "Boy, did he have that coming," Ysa says between giggles.

"No way!" Chen crows, picking himself off the ground. "You did not just do that. Baby Anagram grew a pair!"

Ana can't believe it—*actually, no, I totally can*—but he's coming at her with his hand up and clenched . . . not for a return punch, apparently, but for a fist bump.

She groans. "Is it too late to send him back?"

"Mount Fahr," Chen says, sliding past her without missing a beat, peering over into the pit. "Best lava dipping spot in the universe!"

"What?" Ana says.

"Sure! Put on the right gear, and you can shimmy right down the side, here." He kicks his boot at the patch of ground by his feet. On closer look, it appears that some obstructions have been cleared away and the earth deliberately packed down to make a wide, smooth area surrounding a flat boulder that's embedded in the lip of the crater. It all looks quite intentional, but how could Chen know about this?

"Chen . . . ," Ysa says softly.

Something clicks into place in Ana's mind.

She'd assumed that he knew so much about the planet from having researched it ahead of time. But now . . . "You've been here before," Ana says slowly. "Or . . . all along? Were you already here before us? Is that it? You *weren't* on that rocket?"

Chen looks at her with a suddenly wide-open and vulnerable gaze. He glances behind her at the others. For a second she thinks he's going to speak, he opens his mouth even, shakes his head a little as if he's going to let slip something he knows he shouldn't. But then he takes an involuntary step back.

And the world falls apart.

Ana's watching as it happens and still she can't explain it. He's on solid ground, his feet flat on the embedded rock. And then, suddenly, he's not.

Chen topples into the lava pit.

Ana screams and drops to her belly, desperately trying to see through the searing fumes and smoke. At first she can't see Chen at all. Then there's a low moan down to her left, and she sees him.

Chen has landed on a rocky outcropping about ten feet down, his left leg twisted under him.

"Oh, no," Ysa says, dropping down next to Ana. "Chen! Get up!"

He's struggling to stand, but something about his face scares Ana. His eyes are so wide they look almost totally white, and his breath is coming in short, harsh bursts. Chen isn't just in pain, and he isn't just afraid. He's flat-out terrified.

"We have to do something," Todd says, crawling up to Ana's other side.

"Why isn't he saying anything? It's like he can't hear us calling," Ysa says.

"Grab my legs," Ana says to Todd. "Drop me over the side."

Todd chokes on a mouthful of fumes. "Are you crazy? What are you going to do down there?"

She grabs his wrist and snaps, "It can't be more than a ten-foot drop. Look at him—he's not getting himself out anytime soon. Take my feet. I'll catch hold of him and you pull me back up."

Todd shakes his head but scoots behind Ana and grabs her feet. Ysa scrambles behind Todd to give him extra ballast. As soon as his grip tightens around her ankles, Ana walks her hands over the rim of the crater and down the side. She wishes she'd thought to tie a cloth around her face; the fumes are almost unbearable and the farther down she goes, the less she can see.

"Chen," she calls. "Talk to me! Are you okay?"

"Alex!" he shrieks suddenly, then whimpers, "No, wait. . . ."

Ana is just an arm's reach away when he shrieks again, incoherently this time. He jumps to his feet, knocking into her.

From the rim above, Ana hears Todd yell, "Hey!" Then his hold is gone and Ana crumples down onto the ledge at Chen's feet. She feels her shoulder pop back out of place and bites her lip against the pain, forcing herself to scramble right up to her feet.

"Chen," she gasps, but he seems to have no idea she's there.

"Not the fire, Alex." His head swivels slightly from side to side.

Ana leans in closer and grabs Chen's shoulders. "Look at me," she pleads. "It's Ana. Come on, Chen."

His eyes lock on hers and widen. "What do you want me to do?"

"Just focus, okay?"

A wisp of smoke drifts between them. "I can't do this, Alex. Please don't make me."

What is he talking about? Ana shakes him. "Chen!"

He thrashes from side to side, pulling out of her grasp and taking a step backward on the ledge. "No, please . . . I won't say a word. Just let me go!"

His whole body is shaking, and even though he's talking

right to her, it's obvious that he's not seeing her at all. "Alex," he whimpers. "Not the fire, Alex. No, please, not the fire—I can't. . . ."

Ana forces her voice to remain steady. "It's me, Chen. It's just Ana. You're safe—what you're seeing"—she swallows—"it isn't real. Chen?"

And then for one second his eyes refocus and he's looking right at her. "It's like peace, Ana. It's not giving up. Just letting go." With those words, Chen lifts his arms up and out to each side. He steps back.

"Chen, wait, what are you—"

He takes another step, this one onto open air, but he shows no surprise at finding no ground under his feet. Instead he just gives a sad smile as he topples, straight-backed, toward the fiery abyss below. Ana screams and lunges for him. As she drops to the edge, hands outstretched, the smile stays on his face until even that is swallowed up by the smoke and the fiery darkness.

Chen is gone.

For a long time, all she can do is lie flat on the ledge, body shaking. She can't cry, she can't even speak. Over and over again, she sees Chen fading into the gassy mist, that smile of resignation on his face. After a while, though, the sound of yelling breaks through her grief, and she realizes that it's been coming from overhead for quite a while.

She looks up and thinks for a moment that her mind is

playing tricks on her. Todd's hand is just above her, and he's in her light again, just like he was back at the basin wall when she was fleeing the worm for the first time.

Then she sees Ysa behind him. Their faces are filled with pain and concern and horror, and they're so real and alive that her eyes fill with tears. She is flooded with an urgent desire to live, to move, to go on. Everything that Chen is no longer able to do.

Ana climbs to her feet and slowly scales the wall until she can grab Todd's hand. His grip is strong in hers, pulling hard as she scrabbles with her feet on the rock face. Slowly, slowly she rises out of the steaming pit and collapses next to the others onto the flat, desolate summit of Mount Fahr.

They lie there panting, all three of them, for long minutes. Ysa is crying quietly.

"What happened down there?" Todd asks. "We couldn't really see through all the fumes."

"Something spooked him. He was terrified, Todd. I have no idea why or what caused it, but it's almost like . . . he got scared to death." She knows it sounds ridiculous, but it's what keeps coming into her head when she thinks of Chen's face— right up until the end, of course.

Todd sits up straight. "What do you mean? What was he so freaked out about?"

"I don't know," Ana says, eyes closed. "He didn't know me. He was just raving on about some kind of a fire. He kept calling me Alex."

"A fire?" snaps Ysa, then just as quickly starts sobbing again. "Why would he be talking about that?"

"He was gone somewhere in his head. That's all I know. And then he just—fell. He let himself fall. He didn't slip or anything." Ana goes quiet, and the others don't press her for any more details.

There's something bugging her about this exchange, though, and in the quiet that follows her retelling, it suddenly becomes clear. That glazed look in Chen's eyes, the palpable fear— she's seen it somewhere before. It's exactly the look Todd had when he was in the Dead Forest. When he was stuck in that terrified trance. But what connection could there possibly be? The forest is miles away.

Todd breaks into her thoughts then by climbing slowly to his feet. His face is grim and his look flat. "We should probably keep moving."

Ana sighs. As horrible as it seems to think rationally after what just happened, she knows he's right. Eight hours left to go, and who knows what else is going to come at them on this forsaken planet? "Yeah," she says, pushing herself up. "I guess so."

"Ysa," Todd says slowly as the other girl struggles into her pack. "Does this . . . change anything? About, you know, all the stuff we're not supposed to know?"

Ysa gives him a long look. Then she drops her eyes and shakes her head. "No. If anything . . ." She shrugs. "Let's just keep moving."

Todd nods and shoulders his own pack.

Ana can't bring herself to care. What does it really matter? They just need to get where they're going. Stay safe until then. *Survive.* Those instructions are taking on a whole new meaning, somehow. She bites her lip.

The three of them turn their backs on the pit, and once again Ana fights back tears. She can't erase Chen's face from her mind. She feels a touch on her arm and looks down to see Todd's hand gripping her lightly. "You know you did everything you could for him, right? What happened to Chen"—he swallows—"is not your fault."

Not your fault. There's something in those words that drives a white-hot poker through her belly, and for a second there's a flash in her mind and she's back at the grave, watching the dirt trickle down. . . . She shakes herself.

Brushing Todd's arm aside, she pushes ahead of the others and starts across the wide, flat summit toward the far edge where they will make their descent. Toward the ocean, toward the colony, yes—but above all, away. Away from Chen and loss and madness and piercing slivers of memory that burrow into her broken mind and don't let go.

As far away as she can get.

TWELVE

00:07:58:21

The summit is wider across than Ana had expected. But the pace she sets to cross it helps push some of the storm clouds out of her head. By the time she clears the far side of the peak, the fist in her chest has loosened slightly and she's able to lean over, put her hands on her knees, and catch her breath.

When Ysa approaches, her eyes are fixed on the distant view, her face a mask of wonder. "Oh!" she whispers. She reaches for Ana's arm and squeezes. "Just . . ."

The Maraqa Sea is like a glassy jewel, green and glimmering in the glow of the twin suns. Stretching to the edge of the pink horizon, it steals Ana's words and makes quick tears spring to her eyes. It feels so strange to find this beauty here, so much at odds with the ugliness she has just seen. It can't begin to make up for everything else. But . . .

But maybe, she thinks, looking out across the sea to far-off scattered brown dots that must be islands. *Maybe it's a start.* She wouldn't call it a sign of hope—she's not nearly that sentimental. But with this image of beauty to hold on to, maybe, she thinks, she can continue going forward.

Todd comes up behind them and Ana turns to give him her best I'm-holding-it-together smile. He exhales visibly. "Okay," he says. "Okay, good."

"Can we see the settlement from here?" Ana asks. "The colony?" The last discussion on this subject left a sour taste in her mouth, but that's still their goal, the place where answers lie.

Todd seems unsure, looking off into the distance with brows furrowed. "I don't think so," he says.

Ysa waves an arm toward the distant shoreline, pointing off to the right. "It's a little farther down the coast that way. Can't see much from here."

Ana contemplates the distance they have yet to cross. The sea is there, lapping the far horizon. Before this is a wide wasteland that she remembers from the map as a stretch of sand dunes. Before that is the mountain slope, rolling and tame at its base but growing steeper the higher it gets.

And immediately below them? The mountain just . . . drops away. Ana smiles.

"How . . ." Following the direction of Ana's gaze, apparently, Ysa says with a quavering voice, "How are we going to get down *that?*"

Ana snaps into take-charge mode; something about the

mountain face draws it right out of her. She reaches behind her to pat the side of her pack. "We'll be fine right here. We've got all we need and more," she says.

"We'll be using ropes, I guess," Todd says. He's already shrugging off his backpack, opening it up and looking for gear.

"Third pocket from the bottom left. There's at least one compression block in there," Ana says, distracted. There's a faint flicker in her middle and she's cupping both hands around it to keep it going and growing; she doesn't know exactly what it means but she knows that it's all her and it's all good. And anything remotely good right now has to be grabbed hold of with both hands.

Todd finds the brown rectangular lump of compressed rope and tosses it to her, then shuffles around in the pack a little more. "There's only one—though I guess we've each got one if we need more."

"This should be plenty," Ana says, picking at the opener tab. "It makes, what, fifty feet of rope? A hundred?"

"Ninety-five," Ysa says.

Todd buckles his pack shut again as Ysa eyeballs the drop. "It'll be enough," she says with a shudder. "The length, anyway."

The tab finally gives and Ana tugs at the bristle of rope sticking out. She pulls on it until she has enough rope to wind around her hand. Then she closes her fingers around the coil, holds it tight, and gives the compression block a good strong shake.

With a gentle *pfft*, folds of rope start blooming out of the postcard-sized block, changing its shape like a sponge filling with water. In seconds a scattered coil of rope is lying at their feet.

Todd picks up the end and studies it. He nods approvingly. "It's the good stuff," he says. "No knockoffs for these planetary explorers."

"You have the anchor?" Ana asks.

He nods and tosses her a flat shiny disk, which she catches in her free hand. She studies the rocks around her and finds a smooth, flat area with no cracks or crumbling bits. She runs her hand along it to check for soft spots. Finding none, she puts a hand on either side of the anchor and breaks it neatly in half.

"Have you used one of these before?" she calls over her shoulder.

"Sure," Ysa says, but there's a wobble in her voice.

Ana doesn't need to wonder if she herself has used one. A series of flashes goes off inside her head: rocks and cliffs and clean, biting air; muscles straining; adrenaline pumping; hands red with rope burn; the feeling of power and mastery painting every dull edge bright.

Ana smiles. *Bring it.*

Slipping one half of the anchor into a pocket, she slaps the flat edge of the other half onto the rock. Even before it makes contact, she registers the strong, almost magnetic pull between the rock and the anchor. She tugs on the anchor once it's set; it doesn't budge. It's as if it were growing out of the rock. Good. The bond is strong.

These movements are more than memory; they're rich with the feelings she had when she first saw the mountain. This is knowledge. It's hardwired inside her.

"You want me to take the first swing down?" Todd asks.

"Go ahead," Ana says, sliding the loop of rope off her hand and pressing it around the anchor. She tucks the edges in until they disappear behind the silvery half-disk, then places her palm flat on the anchor and pushes down until the metal warms.

"Did it seal?" Todd asks. There's a tremor in his voice. This descent seems to be putting him and Ysa out of their element. Ana feels like she's just finding hers.

"Yes. It's all set."

He nods and moves into position on the ledge. Leaning down, he presses an indentation on the side of each of his boots, and climbing spikes spring out from the toe and the bottom. There's a second's pause as he circles the rope around his waist. Any hesitation Ana might have sensed disappears as Todd starts down without so much as a nod of farewell.

And why should he? It's just a mountain descent.

Just scaling down a mountain face on the far side of the universe.

Ana squats next to the cliff edge and watches as Todd rappels down, getting smaller and smaller. A few minutes later, he lands safely on a wide ledge.

"Come on!" he calls up.

Ana turns to Ysa. "You're next," she says. She can't wait until Ysa gets herself over the side and down the mountain, because suddenly it's like nothing exists but Ana and this climb, and every moment separating her from it passes with agonizing slowness.

Ysa takes considerably longer than Todd, or maybe it just seems that way, but finally it's Ana's turn. She checks to make sure the rope is still secure, then loops it around her waist. She pops out her own spikes and kicks her boots against the rock, hears the satisfying *clink* that will steady her on the way down the rock face.

This is it!

The second she launches over the side, though, she is jerked back to reality. Whatever her muscles used to be, whatever they are in her head, real life is a little different. The rope hugs her close and she has a strong grip on either side, but—*oh*, her shoulder is on fire. Her body pulses with pain as every bruise and injured muscle from her journey so far flares to life. Feeling fine while walking is apparently not the same as rappelling down a mountain face.

It takes all her effort to keep her breathing level and measured, to keep her hands sliding along the rope and her feet moving down the rock wall.

Still, the rush of the measured drop is glorious. It echoes the thrum of her heart, the pounding in her ears. It's freefall, it's the wind tossing her like a plaything, it's stamp and push and strain and release and flow. It's freedom. It's ninety seconds of pure adrenaline heaven.

And then she's on the ledge, collapsing in a heap as Todd takes the call part of the anchor from her and wraps it in the end of the rope, sending the release charge traveling up to the other end. The whole thing comes tumbling down around them.

She shuts her eyes for a moment, replaying the experience in her mind, loving just being here. "This is what I am made of," she whispers to herself. Whatever this is, it's inside her, whether she's aware of it or not.

This is me.

Cause of Fatalities Not to Be Released in Mass Deaths of APEX1 Crew

Global News Syndicate

The International Astronomical Union (IAU) issued a statement early this morning attributing the deaths of seven members of APEX1, the first group of interstellar travelers to the planet Paradox, to human error. While no details have been released, the IAU stated that the single surviving colonist who returned early last month has been cleared of any suspicion in the deaths. The survivor, whose name has not yet been released, remains under observation for undisclosed health reasons.

"Rumors attributing the deaths to an alien virus or parasite are completely unfounded," said Kimberly Farley, IAU chief media spokesperson. "The Global Infectious Disease Group has given our returning colonist a clean bill of health." The GIDG recently published an investigative report analyzing all available data from the mission. Their findings show that the deaths were not caused by environmental or infectious agents.

A source inside Savitech has confirmed that talks are already under way planning for the launch of a second expedition to Paradox sometime in the next two decades.

THIRTEEN

00:05:40:36

After the mountain's sheer drop-off from the summit, the rest of the descent seems tame by comparison. Mount Fahr rolls out its smoothest inclines and puts plenty of footholds in their path, as if they've passed some test and can now settle into the easy stuff. In less than two hours they are down the slope and crossing the last grassy stretch before they get to the dunes that link the mountains and the sea.

In a strange way it's hard to move on, and Ana can't help sneaking a look behind her, reveling in the sense of power and mastery she found on that rocky slope. Another part of herself reclaimed . . . in spite of the mountain's nearly unbearable price.

She recoils from that train of thought. The only thing they

can do is keep going—three now instead of four, but still moving forward.

Ahead of them lie the rolling purple-blue sand dunes. Ana's about to pull up her map to calculate the distance, but Todd has already activated his, lining it up against the horizon.

"There can't be more than a couple hours to go once we hit the dunes," he says, and she sees him frown at the circlet.

The plan is to chart a course directly across the sand at its shortest possible point, then head down the coast for a half mile or so to reach the end, the goal, the big red X on the map.

With renewed energy, they set off across the last sloping stretch of land toward the dunes. The ground is scrubby with undergrowth and dotted with rough boulders. Ysa walks hunched over, like she's carrying a physical weight. She's hardly spoken a word in the last hour. Every time Ana looks in her direction, Ysa starts to catch Ana's eye, as if the other girl is wrestling with herself, trying to decide if there's something she wants to say. But she never quite comes out with it, and Ana can't bring herself to press her.

As they trudge on, Ana can't stop thinking about the look on Chen's face as he fought for his life on the ledge. Even taking into account the horror of the moment and all that came with it, there was something eerie, something significant about his struggle, which Ana can't quite put her finger on.

Because the bottom line is that Chen didn't *have* to die. He wasn't killed by the fall, or the lava, or any kind of accident or twist of fate. At some point, paralyzed by his fear, lost in whatever twisted vision held him, he *chose* that fate. He was so terrified . . . and then he wasn't anymore. *It's not giving up, just letting go,* he'd said. But why would he do that? What is she missing?

There's the worm to think about, too. They haven't seen slime nor scale of it since taking refuge in the caves. Ana can't really believe it's gone for good, though the more time passes, the more some part of her starts, tentatively, to hope.

"I wonder if there's more than one of those worms," Todd says, as if reading her mind.

"I don't think so," Ana says. "And honestly, something about it just doesn't make sense. There's no animal life on this planet. What does it eat? How does it survive?"

Todd shakes his head. "Maybe plants? Something in the soil?"

Behind them, Ysa scoffs. "Those rows of teeth weren't made for eating plants," she says.

Ana nods. "Exactly. Todd, you said there was evidence that kind of creature existed in prehistoric times. And yet now here it is, back from extinction or something."

"Or something," Todd mutters.

"Well, what's it doing here now?" Ana says. "Plus it wasn't visible on the planet scans. Those letters we found before we left the rocket. They asked us to keep our eyes peeled for things that are out of the ordinary. The worm is a pretty good candidate, don't you think?"

"I'll say," Ysa hisses, and Ana is shocked at the bitterness in her voice. "This whole trek pretty much fits the bill for 'out of the ordinary,' wouldn't you say, Todd? Does that make it a success?"

"We just need to ride this out, Ysa," Todd says levelly. "Don't forget the countdown—there's not much time left."

Ana shivers. Not quite four hours . . . but that should be plenty, right? The suns are both high in the tangerine sky by now, so much closer together than the last time she looked. And the sand dunes are just ahead—one more gentle slope to go, and then they're practically there.

"Yeah, because everything else on this trip has gone so smoothly." Ysa snorts.

Ignoring her, Todd says, "The worm is out of the ordinary in more ways than one." He circles wide to go around a boulder, then falls back in line next to Ana. "That time in front of the cave, after I fell . . . I don't know. I looked up at that monster and suddenly it was like I didn't even care that I was in danger. I should have been running for my life, but I couldn't even move. Didn't want to."

"It's like that every time the worm appears, isn't it?" Ana says. "When it gets close enough or we look directly at it." Ana thinks back to that moment when she knocked Todd aside—she, too, had been frozen in front of the worm, mesmerized by its blank, bottomless eyes and oddly sweet breath. She must have looked just like the others did when the worm first appeared at the base of the mountain—glazed eyes, mouth hanging open. Empty. Disconnected.

Something drops into place in Ana's mind.

That trance-like stare, zoning out and being incapable of motion—that's not just something that happens when the worm is around. That also describes exactly the way Todd nearly got trapped in the Dead Forest, and the way Chen lost his life in the lava pit. The only difference is that their mind screens weren't blank or empty—they were experiencing some kind of hallucinations, horrible memories or nightmares or something.

"I don't know," Ana mutters. "There's some connection with the worm, but I just can't figure out what it is." After all, the worm hadn't been anywhere nearby in the Dead Forest, or on the summit of Mount Fahr. Still. There's no way that could be a coincidence. *It's like peace,* Chen said. That describes the worm's lure exactly. What does it all mean?

"And here we are," Ysa suddenly says. "Meet the purple sand dunes. Can you think of any worse terrain to cross?"

The landscape before them is, more than anything else, flat. It stretches out in every direction, sometimes rising gradually into low dunes, and looking for all the world like a dark sandy ocean. The sunslight paints the dunes a deep purple, like liquid twilight, a sharp contrast to the bright sky.

"A few things before we head out," Todd says, grabbing Ana's arm. "It's not exactly quicksand, but . . ."

"Not exactly?" Ana freezes in place, gazing down at the oddly molten-looking surface. "What does *that* mean?"

"The sands here are unstable," Todd says. "But it's not

125

dangerous. The basin's no farther down than a foot or two, at its deepest. But it's the devil to get loose if you start sinking. So you've just got to keep your steps light. Like this."

Todd takes a slow-motion step onto the surface, his foot settling onto the sand in a smooth arc. "Feet down flat, see?" he says. "First one, then the other, one clean movement. No pointed toes, no heels, and make sure your weight is centered. As smooth and even as you can. Keep it like this, and you might as well be walking on solid ground."

His movements are something between a robot and a tight-rope walker, achingly slow and symmetrical. Ana remembers the thrill of ownership she felt when tackling the mountain; this is obviously Todd's element, as that was hers.

"Just watch out for sudden movements," Ysa says from up ahead. For all her earlier distaste, she is navigating the terrain like a pro. "I hate sand on principle, but I've never had any trouble with this one."

Ana struggles to keep her face neutral, hoping not to show how creeped out she is. Then again, her whole world seems to be made of quicksand today, wide and vast and unrecognizable, filled with lurking dangers just waiting to tug her under.

No. Not under; not here, anyway.

Truthfully, it doesn't look too hard, and Ana would rather look idiotic than end up stuck in some kind of sand trap, shallow or not. Flinging her arms out wide, she puts her weight first on one leg, then the other. The sand under her feet is firm but supple, like walking on a giant water balloon. It takes some concentration at first, but it isn't long before she gets the hang of it, striding along in robot tightrope walker–fashion next to Todd, with Ysa leading the way between the dunes.

"The weird purple color comes from the volcanic rock, or maybe powdered lava," Ysa says, slowing her pace to walk alongside Ana and Todd. "No one knows for sure. Some people think there are deposits of precious stones at the bottom that are ground up by the constant movement of the sand. They think that's where it gets its bluish tinge."

"How long have you been here?" Ana says softly.

"Way too long," Ysa snaps.

After a while the sameness of the landscape starts to wear on Ana, and it's increasingly hard to keep from getting disoriented. Pulling up the map, she finds a point in the distance, a hilly outcropping, and fixes her eyes on that spot. She should probably leave the map up, but the texture of the sand alone is making her a little nauseated. A jostling electronic display would push her all the way over the edge.

She sneaks a glance at Todd, but all his attention is on the sand as he moves into the lead with smooth, easy strides. He's obviously not worried, or at least he isn't showing it.

Ana picks up her pace, speeding up even as Ysa seems to be slowing down.

"Good technique," Todd says, half glancing over his shoulder to flash Ana a grin. "You're as smooth as butter."

For some reason this makes her heartbeat quicken, and she

feels her cheeks heat up. *Focus, Ana.* She keeps her eyes on the midnight-colored sand. Swish, lean, step. Swish, lean, step.

"This isn't so bad," she says.

Glancing down, something catches her eye. Her boots' soles have softened and expanded, even curling up around her feet a little, like tiny surfboards. She had expected the climbing spikes, but this adaptation catches her by surprise.

"Sandshoes," she says. She wonders if the boots can adapt themselves to any surface, or if the shoe designers anticipated these obstacles in particular. For some reason, a cold shiver runs down her spine.

Todd is way ahead by now. Glancing back, Ana sees that Ysa is a full twenty feet behind and standing completely still. She can't quite tell from this distance, but it looks as if the other girl is crying.

"Hey!" Ana calls to her. "Are you all right?"

Ysa nods and moves forward in increasingly jerky steps. "Go on, I'm fine."

"I can wait," Ana says, shifting to balance her body weight as she faces backward.

"What's up?" Todd calls out.

Ysa's face is a mask. She looks like a person hanging at the edge of a precipice, fighting with everything she has just to hold on for another second. Then something in her eyes changes.

She goes over the edge.

Ana sees it happen, watches Ysa's eyes glaze all the way

over, and with a horrible certainty Ana knows what's going to happen next. Ysa's breath starts coming in quick gasps, and a light beading of sweat starts on her face. She stumbles, takes a jerky step, and the toe of her boot plunges down into the sand. Almost instantly, Ysa starts to sink.

Moving smoothly and steadily, Ana heads back for the other girl, practicing at speed the motions she was inching through only moments ago. "Hold on!" She pants. "Don't move!"

Ysa's not moving. Her eyes are wide and staring, still unfocused. *Just like Chen's, just like Todd's in the Dead Forest, but why here? What's going on?* As Ana watches, still moving back toward her as quickly as she can, Ysa sinks several more inches. The sand is now trickling into the tops of her boots, and still she's going down. The sand around her body begins whirlpooling in on itself, sucking inexorably downward.

Ana hears shuffling behind her and knows that Todd has started working his way back to them as well.

"Ysa," Ana says as she reaches her. "Look at me."

Ysa's eyes are rolling wildly in her head now, but Ana can see her making an effort to focus. The sand is nearly up to Ysa's knees, and she seems to be sinking faster. Todd said the basin ended a couple feet down . . . how much longer until Ysa reaches the foundation? When she hits bottom, maybe she can just push off and propel herself back out.

Ana takes Ysa's hands, and Ysa responds with a squeeze of her own. She starts whispering, and Ana leans in closer. "They told me not to jog alone after dark." Ysa's voice is electric with fear. "But the field by the high school always seemed so safe. It was just . . . the one time."

The fear is real, but this isn't some hallucination. This is something real she's remembering.

"The bleachers . . . ," Ysa whimpers. The sand is traveling up her thighs now. *Where is that rock bottom?* "He isn't there and then suddenly he is . . . he . . . holds me down . . . my face is in the dirt. . . ."

Something real she's . . . *reliving.*

The sand seeps past Ysa's waist. Where is Todd?

"Lean into me," Ana says, bending at the waist and holding on to Ysa's arms. "Try to stay still. That way you'll stop sinking, and Todd and I can lever you out. This place isn't dangerous, do you remember that? You know that."

Ysa barks out a laugh, her eyes clearing for a moment as she focuses on Ana. "*You know?* You don't know anything, Ana Ortez."

Ortez. "Is that my name?" Ana asks. "Ysa, is that my last name?"

"We weren't supposed to tell you anything," Ysa moans, "but now it's all—" She jerks suddenly and thrashes her head violently to the side. "Dirt . . . in my mouth . . . so much pain . . . and the weight crushing me. I can't stand it!"

"Don't move a muscle," Todd whispers in Ana's ear, and Ana relaxes just a bit. Todd circles around and takes one of Ysa's arms as the sand begins pooling around her chest. Ana takes the girl's other arm, and they tug, once and then again, pulling at Ysa, who has stopped struggling altogether.

But who has not stopped sinking.

"Todd, what the hell is going on?" Ana says. "I thought you said the basin wasn't deeper than two feet!"

Todd is shaking his head. "It's not, Ana, I swear to you. I don't know what's going on, but this isn't right. This shouldn't be happening."

"Well, what do *we* know?" Ana says, feeling the frantic edge of hysteria as the sand approaches Ysa's neck. "We know nothing, Todd, because we have freaking amnesia! Ysa, come on—look at me."

But Ysa is sunk deep into her nightmare, raving, lost. She lets out one last cry, then jerks back, yanking her fingers out of their grasp.

Her wide, staring eyes are the last thing Ana sees as Ysa disappears into a dark purple whirlpool.

FOURTEEN

00:03:03:18

For a long time neither Ana nor Todd can move. It all went wrong so quickly, it's almost too much to comprehend. Chen's death, and now Ysa's . . . Ana feels as if something inside her has shattered beyond all repair. She keeps running over the scene in her mind, trying to figure out what she should have done differently. Surely there's something, *something* she could have done to change the outcome.

Ysa!

The palpable fear in Ysa's eyes still chills Ana's blood. Ysa's death was too eerily similar to Chen's to be written off as chance. Yet there's no obvious connection that she can see.

And something else . . . is it only a matter of time before she and Todd share the same fate as the others?

Ana realizes that Todd is shifting cautiously on the sand next to her. He extends his hand to her, but she brushes it aside. She doesn't need help, not his and not anyone's. All she needs right now is to keep moving. But no matter how fast she moves, no matter how far she goes, the one thing she can't get away from is herself.

It's so easy to look at the broken pieces of her life and assess who she is when there's so little of it to review. And the more she looks, the more she hates what she sees: cheap muscle and a rabid need for control, a broken mind and a body constantly in motion. What good is any of that to her or to anyone else? What good did it do when she couldn't save the people nearest her?

What kind of person *was* she, once upon a time, before everything went so wrong?

It doesn't matter. Nothing matters now except reaching inside herself and gluing those broken pieces back together into whatever *she wants to make herself*. She can't waste any tears, not inside or out. Rage will be her glue, rage at this planet and at whoever messed with her mind.

There are less than three hours left on the countdown, and as anticlimactic as meeting that deadline might be after Ysa's and Chen's deaths, it's something concrete, something she can turn her mind toward.

The mission must continue.

She sets off across the dunes and Todd shuffles next to her. Above them, the stretch of bruised sky between the suns is shrinking steadily as Torus approaches Anum on its preset collision course. Well, not collision, exactly—though somehow, even that wouldn't surprise her. Is there anything on this alien world that *isn't* set to self-destruct?

Ana keeps to shallow, jerky movements, half daring herself to trigger the sinking mechanism, half believing she deserves the same fate as Ysa because she just stood there—*stood there and wasn't able to save her*—while she died. Just like she couldn't save Chen.

There's some deep core of darkness on this planet, that much is clear. Again she pictures the terror in Ysa's eyes, her whispered words. It was as if she was trapped in some horrible memory of her past.

As if she was being forced to relive the worst moment of her life.

Ana frowns and slows to a standstill. Chen's face flashes into her mind again. What if what he was experiencing wasn't just a hallucination—but a *memory*? He kept talking about—talking *to*—someone called Alex. *Not the fire*, he'd said. Just like Ysa kept raving about being trapped under the bleachers by some psycho.

It's as if they really were back inside those experiences. Inside their memories. Is that even possible?

And . . .

"Todd," she gasps in dawning realization. "Do you remember the story you told me from your past . . . something to do with a forest?" She can remember his words exactly, of course. That's the thing about starting fresh; everything you put in the memory stores stays perfectly well preserved. But she wants to hear him say it. She has a horrible feeling that what Todd encountered in the forest was not just a random hallucination triggered by a deep-seated fear of the forest, but rather some kind of internal replay of *his* worst memory, too— just like Chen's. And just like Ysa's. Only he'd managed to survive it. *She'd* helped him survive it. Could that really be it?

But Todd is turning toward her, a strange glint in his eye. "Do you hear something?"

She pauses to listen. "Oh, no!"

The grinding is not close, but there's no mistaking the sound drifting across the dunes.

"It's different this time," Todd says, and his face is a new shade of pale. "Do you hear that? It sounds like the wind, or . . ."

Ana hears the difference, too, but he's completely wrong about what it sounds like. It's more like glass . . . breaking glass? But there's no time for listening or analysis. They need to keep moving.

And so they start off again, trying for haste even though their lives depend on keeping their movements smooth and easy. Swish, lean, step. Swish, lean, step. Any urges Ana had toward self-recrimination are long gone; now it's just a focused fast-forward, slippery fear fueling their steps.

They make swift progress, the only sound their labored breathing and the gentle *swish* of their feet across the sand.

Wait . . . the only *sound?*

Ana stops and cocks her head. "Hey," she whispers.

"It's gone," Todd says, slowing alongside her. "But who knows for how long? We should make as much progress as we can. There's only two hours left to go."

He turns and resumes his shuffle across the sand, toward the splash of ocean that is growing ever more visible up ahead.

Ana follows him, but in the quiet her mind worries at the problem of the worm. Why can't they get away from it? "First the crater, then the mountain, then the sand dunes," she says. "It's always right on us. It doesn't seem to be able to get through extreme land formations—maybe the dunes stopped it this time. But then it just goes and finds another way around. Todd, it's just going to keep coming."

"I have no idea what that thing is capable of," Todd says. "I do know it's getting more terrifying every time we meet it."

"More terrifying," Ana repeats. Because he's right—this last time, there was something new about the worm that she hadn't noticed before. "Todd, what does the worm sound like to you? What do you hear?"

He looks surprised. "Well, grinding, I guess. But this last time there was more—something dark and whispery, like the wind through the trees." He shudders.

Of course. What Todd hears from the worm is the sound of the forest at night. *The forest of his personal nightmare, the nightmare that tried to trap him?* She remembers Chen, the first time he heard the worm, speaking of hearing fire. *Was that what the worm sounded like to you, Chen?* And she, Ana, hears breaking glass. And yet she *has* no memories.

Is this what's kept her from the attacks that paralyzed the others?

And, more importantly, could there really be some kind of connection between the worm and those horrible fear-memories? The effects seem to eerily echo each other—and yet there's no way she can reconcile them together.

"Come on," Todd says, reaching for her hand. And this time it somehow seems right to shuffle closer to him as they swish, lean, step—moving forward, with the waves of purple desert at their backs and the vast sweep of everything they don't know shifting and shaping itself like the sand under their feet.

By the time they reach the end of the dunes, Ana is so bone-weary she almost doesn't register it when the sand just ahead of her gives one last shimmer before fading into mud-brown silt. She looks up, and her eyes fill with tears.

The sea.

Vivid green waves cascade over a rocky shore, stretching off into the distance as far as she can see. She takes the last step off the sand and her legs wobble under her.

Todd grabs her arm. "Steady," he says. "It'll take a few steps to adjust." But he's wobbling, too, and for a second they cling to each other, finding their balance on this newly solid ground. Ana is surprised at the joy that springs up inside her. Immediately she feels like a traitor. How can she be happy—relieved—at putting this behind her when the price was so high?

Her hands are trembling as she lifts her circlet and activates the map. The X is so big and close it's practically glowing. The area around it on the map is colored in dull gray, and as she zooms in she sees that it's labeled APEX. It's the colony; it has to be! From the summit of Mount Fahr it wasn't visible, but now, here it is—barely a half mile down the coast. In the misty spray rising off the ocean, she can just make out a dark bulk that looks like a stone wall.

It's real, an actual human settlement they are *this close* to reaching. Ana looks at her circlet. Half an hour to go. They're going to make it! She looks at Todd and they break into a run.

And that's when she sees it, a dangling sparkle of light at the edge of her vision, drifting down just ahead of her.

"Todd," she says, "do you see that?"

"What the hell *is* it?" Todd whispers.

This twisting, glimmering memory strand is smaller than the first two. It looks somehow loose and patchy, like it's starting to come apart at the seams. Seeing it, Ana feels a moment of hesitation, remembering what she experienced last time.

Yet some part of her craves it. She can still picture Bailey's world as she saw it hours ago, can still feel that deep connectivity of living inside that other mind, even so briefly. She's desperate to know what's happening to Bailey, to her world, sure—but it's more than that. It's like some part of her is fused with Bailey, as if *she*, too, is somehow living this other life.

She has to get back inside.

Ana changes course, dashing off to the side to follow the strand's wind-whipped tumble. Behind her, Todd frantically calls, "Ana! What are you doing? You have to stop—"

It's right above her now, all shimmery-bright, pulsing with *otherness*. Ana reaches her hand to the sky. She closes her eyes. There's an icy gush as the memory strand pools around her fingers and slides down her body.

Ana tumbles into darkness.

Water . . . if only I could have a glass of water. Maybe that would help stop the coughing. But the blood . . . there's so much blood everywhere. This thing is supposed to be inside my head, living in my mind. So why all the blood? Why all the shaking, the chills . . . oh, God, the coughing . . . it hurts!

This disease has spread so quickly. I have to update the report now that I know, now that I really know for sure where things are—

But I can't seem to lift my head off my desk. Not even to look at my watch. Can't do it. Is the night gone? Morning, too, maybe? I don't know.

Brian! How is he doing? Haven't spoken to him in . . .

I laugh suddenly. Jackson would let me go home now, wouldn't he? Quarantine protocols be damned, I suppose, once the world starts coming apart at the seams.

But it's too late now. I can hardly even lift my head.

Maybe it's better this way, going out like this. So many gone already. Who would want to linger? Because of course no one's going to survive this. We know that now.

But I will regret not seeing Brian one last time, not being with him as I . . . as we . . .

"Bailey!" *Pat's calling from his cube, up near the front of the room. His voice sounds like mine feels. Who else is still alive in here? The techs left hours ago. Is there anyone left but us two?*

Oh, God. No! The trials are active. How could I have forgotten about that? It's been hours since I last checked in. I have to . . . oh, God, they have no idea what's going on here. I was supposed to be on call. But there's no time, and I can't—

"Pat!" *My voice is even rougher than before. It's coming undone; I can hardly understand myself. I drag myself across the room and look around the divider into Pat's cube. He's there, hunched over beside his desk. Long gray hair spiked up with sweat. Blood dripping down his face. And the look in his eyes . . . No. He won't see tonight, either. We're a sorry pair.*

Always, the blood. Why does this sickness bring so much blood with it? It's in my head, all in my head. If I could just have a glass of—

Wait . . . where am I? I'm there again . . . I'm back down under. So deep. High above me there's the reflection of light on the surface of the water. I have to get up, get some air! I'm reaching, pulling as hard as I can. But my foot is caught, I'm trapped. I'm trapped!

"Mommy!" *I want to scream.* "Mommy!" *But I can't, I'm underwater and I need to breathe, I have to. I won't be able to hold out any longer and my mouth opens without my permission and water crashes into my lungs and I'm drowning, I'm drowning, and it hurts but it's peaceful, too, and my lungs kick one more time, trying to expel the water—*

No. It's not real.

That happened twenty years ago, and I didn't drown, I was rescued.

It's not happening. I'm in the office, I'm next to Pat's cube, retching and coughing up even more blood.

But the fear . . . that was just as real as the first time. It's the disease, I know that—it's got me on a fear loop and I can't seem to break out. They're all connected somehow . . . the blood and the fear and the pain and . . .

I have to focus. I've got to get to the trials. I've got to find some way to—while I still—if I could just—

Ana's eyes fly open as an electric jolt of panic courses through her body. It's like she's stuck her hand into a socket. Her body goes stiff and rigid, and for one trembling moment there's no air in her lungs. . . .

And then she's back. On the beach, heart hammering, rocky ground under her back.

It's never been like that before. Always the experience fades out as the strand drifts away, but this time she watched, felt, *was* Bailey so horribly sick—Bailey *dying.*

Ana sits up slowly, shakily. Todd is standing above her, his face ghostly, his eyes wide and panicked.

He grabs her hand and helps her to her feet. "Ana, what was that? Did you black out? What happened?"

What is she supposed to say? *I just slipped inside some stranger's head and saw a room filled with death? I just saw—just was—someone named Bailey, lying on the floor, choking on her own blood, in some kind of nightmare world that's maybe in the past, or maybe the future, or maybe all in my head?*

She forces herself to smile. "Everything's okay, I'm back," she says, trying to keep her voice from wobbling. "I'm fine."

"If you're okay, we really need to . . ." As he glances over his shoulder, Ana can hear it for herself. The worm is back—but with less grind and even more glass than last time. She's on her feet so fast her head starts spinning and she has to steady herself on Todd's arm. Then they are off, stagger-running down the beach toward the dark walls of the colony that loom ahead, just up a little bluff.

Overhead, the space between the suns has narrowed to a gash. The sky is a shade of dull pink Ana has never seen before, a hard-biting glare that looks ominous. Somehow it's a perfect fit for this planet as she's come to know it, with its deep core of darkness—the other face of the planet, its true face maybe.

This is the sky that the worm plays under.

The place people come to die.

"We're still going to make it," Ana gasps as they run. "It's going to be okay. There must be weapons or something in there, right? In the colony? Something we can use to fight the worm?"

"Ana." Todd's breathing is labored, too. "There's so much you don't know. . . ."

The words chill her. That *she* doesn't know? What about *him?*

Somewhere to their rear, the worm lets out a shattering roar.

She forces herself to focus on what matters. There must be

houses inside the settlement. Bunkers, maybe? According to Chen and Ysa, nobody knew about the worm before now, but there still has to be some sort of protection. It's an alien planet, after all! Surely they had defenses.

"We just had to get this far!" Todd yells beside her. "And when the time is up, then . . ." His eyes are frantic as he looks at his circlet. "But the worm wasn't supposed to be here."

Ana darts a look over her shoulder. The worm is here, all right—mouth agape, roaring along the beach in a maelstrom of whirling dirt and stone fragments—a couple hundred feet away and closing the distance fast.

Just ahead is the short incline leading to the base of the colony's wall, which is made of piled-up stones fixed with some type of mortar. It's a quick scramble for Ana to get up the bluff. The wall is tall right where she is, but as she runs along following the edge, she sees that parts of it have crumbled down to about eye level, and even lower.

Ana finds a gap where she can look over the wall. Several small dwellings made of flimsy-looking materials lie in a state of complete disrepair—roofs are caved in, walls are cracked, and everything is covered by sand. On the far edge of the settlement she can see the start of a more durable building, stones heaped upon each other in the beginnings of a foundation, a task begun but certainly not seen through to completion.

The colony, if this really was a colony, has not only been deserted for some time, but it looks like the settlers never even finished building it.

Ana takes a step backward, unwilling to believe what she is seeing.

She remembers Chen and Ysa's discussion on the mountain. They said there were a few survivors . . . or did they? Leaving aside all the hedging and half-truths, one thing right now is abundantly clear: this place is abandoned. There are no reinforcements. There is no refuge.

She and Todd are on their own.

In that moment, Ana realizes that she can no longer hear the worm.

She turns and finds that Todd has stopped at the bottom of the slope. Like a knight facing down a dragon, Todd plants his feet wide and stretches his arms out to either side. A long blade glints in each hand. The worm is advancing on him slowly, just like it did at the mouth of the cave, closing in with the surety of predator on prey.

"Todd!" Ana yells. "What are you doing?"

"Stay right where you are," he calls back without turning. "We just need another minute. . . ."

Ana looks up and gasps. There's no more than a hairbreadth of sky left between the suns. She glances at the circlet. Barely a minute until zero hour.

The worm opens its mouth so wide that, for a second, it's nothing but a giant gaping maw. As it roars, the sky goes from a dull peach to an assault of light so bright it feels like it's peeling back Ana's skin. Ana drops to her knees and hides her face against the ground. The light is a crushing physical force.

Somewhere beyond the pain she hears Todd yell, the pounding of running steps, and the crunch of a blade hitting something hard. The worm tackling him? His tackling the worm?

Eyes still shut, Ana scrabbles down the incline and fumbles for the pistol in her vest. She squeezes her eyes open just enough to orient herself. In her peripheral vision, the two suns are meshed into one amorphous glowing ball of fire, reacting somehow to each other's presence in a cascade of fiery sparks and—what? Radiation? Gamma rays? Shielding her eyes with her hands, she struggles toward the worm.

Todd is hanging off the side of the worm's head, one of his daggers hooked into the leathery skin next to the beast's left eye. As she watches, he swings his other arm up and plants his second blade higher on the worm's head.

He's climbing the worm's flank! Ana wonders if he's trying to get to the eyes, or the fleshy-looking area between them.

Ana draws her pistol, aims for the worm's gaping mouth— she doesn't dare risk trying for the eyes, with Todd so near— and fires.

At the sound of the report, Todd looks back over his shoulder at her, eyes wide.

"Get away!" he screams. His grip slips and he catches himself just in time. "Get behind the wall at least! You've got to *survive!*"

Something inside Ana's chest squeezes into a tight ball. She doesn't think she'll be able to stand it if the last word Todd ever says to her is *survive* when he's risking so much.

She's running toward him, looking for a better shot, when she feels a thrum on her wrist. Her circlet is warm and suddenly aglow.

$$00{:}00{:}00{:}18$$

$$00{:}00{:}00{:}17$$

$$00{:}00{:}00{:}16$$

Ana stops, suddenly realizing that the sunsmeet is already here; the colony is empty and in ruins.

So . . . what has the countdown been for?

$$00{:}00{:}00{:}12$$

$$00{:}00{:}00{:}11$$

The worm shakes itself, and Todd crashes to the ground in front of the monster, his left leg bent awkwardly under him. One dagger stays lodged in the worm's hide, a seep of dark liquid dripping in its wake. The other has fallen out of his reach in the sand. Todd looks up at the creature, and even from this distance Ana can tell he's lost to the worm's trancelike pull.

00:00:00:08

"Hey!" Ana screams. "I'm over here!"

00:00:00:06

There's an instant where the worm turns its head to look at her, and she feels the crush of its bottomless stare. Then the worm's tail whips around and smashes into Todd, tossing him into the air like a piece of driftwood.

"NO!"

00:00:00:02

Todd hurtles out toward the sea.

00:00:00:01

The worm bears down on her.

00:00:00:00

Ana's head jerks back as though it's been caught on a fishing hook. There's a tearing sensation, as if someone has hold of her skin and is pulling it off.

Then a sheet falls over her mind and everything goes white.

Part 2

APEX2 Deaths Attributed to Unknown Virus

Galaxy Voice

After the return Sunday of the shuttle containing just eleven survivors out of the sixteen original APEX2 colonists, scientists can no longer rule out the possibility of an alien virus. "We are focusing every effort on analyzing the available information, and are confident that we will soon be able to make our findings public," said Dr. Rick Paolo of the Global Infectious Disease Group. The returning colonists are being held in an undisclosed quarantine facility, and reports confirm that several among them are now also showing signs of infection.

"There is some evidence that an infectious entity may have been carried back from Paradox by the APEX2 survivors," admitted Dr. Paolo, stressing that the disease has been fully contained and there is absolutely no danger to the public. Crew members of APEX2 were not available for comment.

In an ironic twist, the most controversial part of this space mission—the inclusion of teenage crew members from Savitech's prestigious ExtraSolar Youth Science program—has delivered a hopeful result. A source inside Savitech confirms that the only crew members showing no signs of infection are the four teenagers.

FIFTEEN

This is how she wakes. There is a heavy pressure on her chest and a dull weight in her legs. Her mouth feels like cotton, and her eyes are glued shut.

No . . . not glued. She thinks they might open, if she tries. She tries.

Everything is white. And somewhere nearby, a very faint sound: *beep . . . beep . . . beep . . .*

To her left there's a wall and to her right a paneled screen. Overhead, fluorescent lights shine from a painted ceiling.

Where am I?

Lights . . . a ceiling . . . She's indoors, lying on a bed. But how?

She remembers the worm . . . the overlapping suns . . . the end of the countdown . . .

And then nothing.

What's happened to me?

Ana tries to sit up, but there's something on her forehead, holding her down. There's a wide strap across her hips. And when she tries to lift her arms, she finds them restrained, too. Ana forces herself to take slow, steady breaths. *One thing at a time.*

She wiggles her arms, which slide easily out of the loose restraints. Then she brings her hands up to her head, feeling a thick band across her forehead. Fumbling a little, she finds a button, which she depresses. The band splits open and falls off to either side of her head. As it pulls away she hears little suction sounds coming from her forehead, as if a series of connections is coming loose.

A second time Ana tries to sit up. This time she gets halfway before the room begins to spin. Black spots lace her vision.

She drops back onto the bed.

I need to take it easy, slow things down. Even though that's the last thing she feels like doing.

She touches her tongue to her lips and discovers they are sandpaper rough. So she's been here awhile. Unconscious. *Captive?*

Trying to steady her pounding heartbeat, she starts over. She moves slower this time, easing herself gradually to a sitting position. But there's still that band on her hips. She realizes after a moment what it reminds her of: the belt on her seat, back inside the rocket. But a cluster of wires and cords snake out of this belt and twine away below the bed.

Under her trembling fingers, the band comes apart as easily

as the one on her forehead did. And sure enough, just like back in the rocket, rows of acupuncture-like needles withdraw from her midsection, leaving a dull, pulsing ache.

So wherever she is, they've got equipment. Technology. And for some reason, her bodily needs have been taken care of—fluids, elimination, nourishment.

But why am I still alone?

Ana looks down at her body. Her jumpsuit is gone. She's wearing jeans and a tight cream-colored shirt with long sleeves and a red embroidered flower pattern. Somehow she knows that the jeans are Olive brand size 29, and on the shirt there's a—no, that's ridiculous. But Ana lifts the hem of the shirt anyway.

Just above the stitching is a wide green stain, which looks an awful lot like grass.

It *is* a grass stain.

How does she know these things?

Then she notices something else: she's wearing a nametag again—just like the one she removed back in the rocket. It's got the same cheap plastic holder, the same silvery pin. With trembling fingers Ana unclips the little plastic tag. The paper inside is very different from the nearly blank one she saw last time. This tag is ringed by a red border, with small red letters along the bottom: SAVITECH. Above this is a small thumbnail photo of a girl with dark brown eyes and cropped hair and a stony expression. Next to the image is printed: ANA ORTEZ.

Does the girl look familiar? Ana can't say. She looks like

someone out of a dream, someone not quite known but not unknown, either. Bile rises in Ana's throat at the thought that she is looking at her own photograph and she doesn't recognize herself.

What is going on here?

Her head is steadier now and Ana turns her body, very slowly, keeping her left hand on the bed for support. She glances down and freezes in place.

Thick, ropy scars wind over the back of her hand, the backs of both hands—lacing each of her fingers, covering her wrists like vines before creeping under her long sleeves and out of sight.

Whose hands are these?

She doesn't remember these hands—but she knows them. Knows with the rock-bottom solidity that has come with each of her regained bits of knowledge that these are *her* hands, *her* scars, *her . . . guilt?*

The word jumps out at her, but she can't deal with it right now, can't remember, doesn't want to remember. These are her hands, her clothes, her body. That's enough for now.

What really matters is figuring out where she is and what's going on.

She slides her feet off the bed and rests them on the floor. She's wearing white canvas sneakers—no more hiking boots. She tests the injury in her shoulder by shrugging it. Nothing. No pain at all.

How long have I been here?

In front of her bed stands an IV drip with a tube dangling down loose. But the bag that held the liquid is empty, the tube dry. Ana tries to lick her lips again. Is that why she is so parched? Maybe whoever has her here is due to come fill up the device.

Or has given up on keeping her alive.

The room is small, with a narrow space around each side of the bed. And all the equipment . . .

Ana's attention snags on a wide readout panel that fills the head of her bed, like a spider's body with its wire limbs dangling to connect to a wide black band. The band she now knows was fastened around her forehead. So, wires that were connected *to her*. The main face of the panel is a wide display screen. It's gray with static and is also the source of that faint beeping that she's been hearing on the fringes of her awareness.

For a moment Ana wonders what was on the readout before she disconnected herself from it. There's something at the edge of her mind, something she thinks she might remember if she tried hard enough—but right now she's too frantic to try bringing it back. If she even could.

Ana stands, pausing just long enough to be sure her legs will hold her—and they do, with just the barest tremble—before shuffling to the end of the bed.

At the far side of the room, to the left of her bed, is a doorway with clear plastic strips hanging from the frame. Across from it, on the right wall, is a heavy door marked EXIT.

Ana contemplates the door with the plastic strips. Why can she suddenly remember the feel of them slapping across her face? Was she carried through them? Did she walk through them on her own? Shaking herself, wishing she could shake some of the cobwebs out of her brain as well, she turns to the heavy door and pushes through.

She finds herself in a large room with office cubicles to one side and a lounge area to the other. A big set of glass double doors lies directly across the room from her, leading into an outer hallway.

Ana steps into the main area and looks around. The air is cooler here, but it smells horrible, a stench like nothing she's ever smelled before. In the lounge area there's a pink velour couch facing a coffee table and a flat-screen television mounted on the wall. The television is on, its screen showing a vacant, pixelated pattern.

Right next to the television is a water cooler. Ana nearly falls on top of it in her relief. She downs five cups of water in quick succession, and the cold liquid helps to settle her thoughts. There has to be a logical explanation for all of this. She just needs to keep looking.

Dropping her cup in the trash, she turns back to face the couch. It's big and soft and suddenly, something about it looms sharp in her mind. There's a spot between the two middle cushions where the springs have bent to the side and left a hiding place. . . .

How do I know that?

Ana is standing over the couch before she realizes she's moved. As her hand slides between the cushions, she already knows what she's going to find.

She pulls out a scrap of paper no bigger than the palm of her hand. Scrawled in blue ballpoint ink is:

O+O

The same message that was scribbled at the bottom of her instructions from the rocket. She pats her shirt where her pocket used to be, but of course the letter is gone, along with her missing jumpsuit.

There's a picture window perpendicular to the couch. Letting the scrap of paper fall to the floor, she moves toward the window. Outside, the sky is not pink or peach or raspberry; it's blue. Dark, midnight blue. There's a single moon, round and full, rising over the edge of a tall building.

There are buildings everywhere. The window she's looking from is high off the ground—ten, maybe twenty stories up. She can see the roofs of buildings all around her, some flat, some shingled, some with little rooftop gardens. There's water in the distance, glinting black in the moonlight.

And electricity. There are streetlights below her.

Federal Street, she knows suddenly. Downtown Boston. Massachusetts.

She isn't on Paradox anymore. She's back on Earth.

She's home.

Ana chokes back a sob. She runs her hands over her face and feels the series of faint depressions on her forehead where the suction marks from the probes and electrodes on her forehead band must have been attached. But the rest of her skin is perfectly smooth and healthy. There's no sign of the deep gouge she received in the Dead Forest. For the wound to have healed so completely . . . how long has she been back?

Once she lost consciousness at the colony, she must have been put immediately into suspended animation and into a rocket home. Four months' travel—*how do I know this, without knowing that I know?*—that should be plenty of time to explain her good-as-new shoulder, the way her other bruises and cuts have faded.

What about her hands, though? Where did all these new scars come from?

Her legs have started shaking and she can't seem to make them stop. She turns from the window and walks toward the television she noticed earlier, its screen still bright and blank. There's a remote on the coffee table and she picks it up, hovering over the *off* command, then she pauses. She slides her finger to the left and scrolls through the channels instead. The next channel shows the same empty display. As does the next, and the next. *What's going on?*

Something has to be connected!

Finally, she finds a channel with a picture. It's a newscast set, a room dominated by a large desk. On the wall behind the desk is a bright logo saying WCN-TODAY. At the bottom of the screen is the flashing red word: *LIVE!*

The picture is tilted ever so slightly, as if someone bumped the camera and didn't bother to fix it. And there are no people in the frame.

Or . . . are there?

Ana leans closer to the screen, then gasps.

The newscaster's desk is empty, but on the floor partly hidden behind the desk a man with black wire-frame glasses is lying on his back, one arm half covering his face.

A face dark with blood.

Ana jerks back from the screen. On live television? Where is the camera operator, where are the lighting technicians, where are the network executives?

And suddenly, she thinks she knows what's going on. There's only one place she can remember seeing that kind of blood, that kind of death: inside a twisting memory strand that rippled across the face of an alien planet.

Her heart sinking, Ana turns to take in the rest of the room. The cubicles that fill the main office area look familiar, and not from some shadowy half-memory. This room, this place— she's seen it recently.

She saw it through Bailey's eyes.

This is the room where Bailey died.

SIXTEEN

Ana steps around the couch and moves toward the rows of cubicles. She follows a narrow walkway through the dividers toward the back of the room.

Bailey walked here, just like this, but how long ago?

Ana passes the sign-up sheet for a lunch that will never be ordered, passes a framed award that no one cares about any longer, passes a fold in the carpet that Bailey tripped over in another world, in another life.

Bailey's desk is pin-neat, with two ballpoint pens placed at right angles to a spiral notebook; a cherry-red cup of congealed coffee sits in the center of a mosaic-tiled coaster; a wide, slim monitor shows a screen full of multicolored fish. On the rim of the monitor is a yellow sticky note with the scrawl: *Call Brian!*

Ana catches her breath and moves inside the cube. The phone is on the right side of the desk, half hidden by the back of Bailey's swivel chair.

On the desk, next to the phone, there is a hand.

Ana moves the chair, and a body—*Bailey's body, still wearing its white lab coat*—tumbles to the floor. Bailey's eyes are wide and fixed. Her long blond curls are stuck to the side of her face and caked with blood.

Ana's heart is pounding like thunder in her ears as she reaches down to touch Bailey's hand. It's stone cold.

She sees now that there are smears of blood everywhere—on the desk, on the chair, on the carpet. Something inside her curls into a tight ball. Not until now was Bailey truly real to her; it's as if Bailey has both come to life and died in the same moment.

Choking back a sob, Ana folds Bailey's arms across her chest, wishing there were something she could do, knowing it's far too late. And also wishing—*selfishly, I know this*—that Bailey could have been alive to tell her what's going. To help provide some answers.

She stands up, and her hip jostles Bailey's desk. The fish swimming across the monitor fade out, replaced by a brightly colored desktop littered with icons. There's a console pocket just below the rim of the desk.

Maybe there's nothing she can do for Bailey. But the answers—*who am I? where am I? what's going on?*—might not yet be out of Ana's reach.

Sliding Bailey's chair to the side—she can't bring herself to sit down in it—Ana kneels in front of the desk and slides both hands into the console pocket. Within the silky inner pocket, magnetic imaging gloves tighten into place around her fingers.

There's a moment of uncertainty while her blank memory wonders what to do, but then her fingers start moving. She knows this. She might not remember it, but her body *knows*.

With barely perceptible movements, Ana reaches into the computer, watching her actions play out on the screen as she sorts through folders. A window pops up with a file list and she scrolls through it. There's so much here, and she has no idea where to start.

She doesn't even know what she's looking for.

She browses, opens, closes, clicks, groans in frustration. There's *too much*! And none of it feels at all relevant.

Giving up on the file list, she pulls up a display of recently activated programs. Something catches her eye: an icon with the image of a tiny planet. The label says PARASIM. Ana selects the program, and it pops up from a minimized window. The program was already running.

The screen erupts with information: lists and coordinates and arrows and features and taglines and buttons. It's obviously a world of work and care and monitoring. But monitoring *what*?

At the top of the window, a pale pink speech bubble is gently flashing. Ana clicks on it, and it opens up a chat window:

<T/O: Is anybody there? Bailey? Where is
     everyone?>

Ana positions the cursor to hover over the T/O, which must signify the originator of the message, and sees TODD OSLOW.

What?

She's looking at the last in a long series of messages. Ana scrolls back up to the top of the window and sees more pale pink bubbles from **TODD OSLOW**, yellow ones from **YSA KLEIN**, and blue ones from **CHEN WAI**.

Ana feels suddenly dizzy. The messages from Todd begin with random updates:

<T/O: Landing successful. All appears
      normal.>

They start to communicate alarm:

<T/O: Something isn't right. There's a
      creature, some kind of giant worm.
      More soon.>

And then there's one that makes Ana's heartbeat go into rapid fire:

<T/O: AO sleeping, stepped out for a quick
      report. Worm threatening viability of
      mission. Need instructions ASAP.>

AO as in Ana Ortez? She thinks about when Todd left her alone in the cave. And he must have found other moments as they traveled together to send in reports. She frowns, thinking of at least one time when he was fiddling with his circlet while they were on the run.

Near the end of the string of messages she sees a series of frantic reports from Ysa:

> <Y/K: Abort mission. Repeat: ABORT!
> Condition of Chen Wai unknown. Send
> update and confirm.>

> <Y/K: Damn it, Bailey, where are you? No
> messages received since 20h. What's
> going on? Are we in danger? Abort
> mission—PULL US OUT, Bailey!>

Ana suddenly realizes something has been nagging at her about the messages: as she clicks on and reads each one, its color changes, going from a creamy pale to a darker, more vivid color.

Nearly half of the messages were unread.

Could it be that Bailey never saw the cries for help? The whole time they were running and fighting for their lives, the whole time Chen and Ysa were dying on some distant planet—and no one knew?

Yet she, Ana, made it back safely from this trip. How did that happen? Who sent her home?

Ana drops her forehead to the desk, forcing herself to breathe slowly in and out. The smell of blood and death fills her nostrils, and her head spins. She needs to focus, and the most important thing she needs to figure out is what's happening here *now*. The planet stuff, her travel, that can wait until later.

For now—why are people bleeding to death?

She thinks back to what she saw of Bailey's experiences, inside those memory strands. There was talk of a sickness on Earth, some kind of disease that was spreading so fast no one was prepared for it. And now apparently the disease has spread and Bailey really is dead. She thinks of Bailey's memory of her coworker Pat, thinks of the newscaster she saw, dead on live television.

Bailey and how many others?

Lifting her head again, Ana shuts down the ParaSim program, leaving the rest of the messages unread. She scans the rest of the icons on the desktop, wondering if there's anything she's missed, knowing there's still vital information she doesn't have.

What sickness is this?

And then she sees it: right in the center of the screen, the icon of a notebook page, topped by a small red flag. Whatever that is, the flag marks it as urgent. She remembers Bailey talking about a report she'd been working on, something she desperately needed to update. Could this be it?

Shifting her hands inside the console, Ana selects the icon and opens up the word processor. The page is topped with large red letters: URGENT AND CONFIDENTIAL.

Hands shaking, Ana scrolls down and begins to read.

TO: Jackson R. Pritchett

FROM: Bailey Sinclair

SUBJ: Analysis of *Vermiletum-V:* Overview of Disorder
     and Newly Increased Infection Risk

Originally thought to be a containable disease,
Vermiletum's recent mutation shows an alarmingly
high threat potential. The prion-based infection
widely referred to by the public as a virus is in fact
a malignant neurological disorder caused when
normal proteins in the brain begin to misfold into
mutated form.

Once triggered, these defective proteins,
or prions, begin to affect the hippocampus,
playing upon the storage and retrieval of long-
term memories. Subsequently spreading to the
amygdala, the infection appears to magnify
memories associated with a strong fear response,
simultaneously amplifying the brain's electrical
activity to hundreds of times its usual strength.

This amplified electrical activity appears
responsible for *Vermiletum*'s highly unusual form
of transmission. The amplification is so strong that
the electrical pulse can reach out to infect nearby
individuals, triggering the misfolding in new victims.
Neural pathways are thus altered to the extent that
these warped biochemical signals can be continually

broadcast out to infect new victims with absolutely no need for physical contact.

As the infection progresses, it activates fear centers in the brain, triggering a release of stress hormones and causing severe panic attacks. The disease inhibits the reuptake of these hormones, preventing them from being absorbed into the body and causing the attacks to continuously increase in length and scope. Other organ systems are subsequently affected, notably the circulatory system, which leads to hemorrhaging in the liver, lungs, and kidneys, resulting in eventual organ failure and finally death.

Because neural pathways in the infected are permanently altered, there has been much speculation in scientific journals that if the infection were successfully reversed in just one patient, that patient's brain would continue to transmit a signal to those nearby, but the signal would shift from one that is warped and infection-creating to one that is balanced and infection-cleansing. The hope is that this would lead to a cascade effect, something like a reverse infection pattern. Unfortunately to date there has been no progress made in understanding how to reverse the infection.

In any event, any hopes for such efforts appear to come too late, as the disease has now morphed into a far more virulent strain, *Vermiletum-V.*

Documented cases of the new variant include a notably decreased incubation period, with first symptoms appearing within hours (rather than weeks) of infection, and strikingly amplified fear responses. The scope of contagion also seems highly accelerated, imprinting the infection in new victims through the most casual of cognitive contact.

Further study and immediate decisive action is necessary if we are to avoid a pandemic of unimaginable proportions.

Ana's pulse is pounding in her ears as she slowly draws her hands out of the console pocket. *Vermiletum*. Just one word, and the cause of so much death and destruction. So that's what happened to Bailey and . . . how many more?

She suddenly, desperately, needs to find someone else, anyone else who is still alive.

Ana jumps up and sprints through the cubicles toward the main door leading out of the office. She pushes through and looks up and down a bright white hallway. Which way? There's a blinking light farther down the hall, and she follows it to an elevator, and a sign that says FLOOR 16.

Ana presses the call button, and after a moment the doors slide open. Stepping inside is like passing for one brief moment into another world, someplace normal, where everything is all right again.

The moment passes.

She pushes G for ground.

The walls of the elevator are mirrored. As the elevator descends, Ana stares at herself, at this wide-eyed, disheveled stranger until she finally can't stand it anymore and turns away. *Stop.* She didn't let herself cry for Bailey; she won't cry for herself.

The doors slide open again, and Ana steps into a brightly lit foyer. It's empty.

Ana's heart starts up a slow, pounding rhythm. She walks across a plush red carpet to a tiled marble floor. Through a revolving glass door she can see the dark outside. Directly opposite the door is a massive mahogany desk, but no one is sitting at it. On one side of the desk is a smaller door marked EMERGENCY EXIT; on the door's white paint is a bright red handprint.

Bailey's blood-streaked face flashes through Ana's mind. Ana turns away from the print, pushes through the revolving door, and steps out into the night.

A cold wind slams into her. She looks up and down the narrow street. It's deserted, and though a row of cars is parked along one side, there's nobody walking or driving nearby. Farther down the street Ana sees the glowing sign of a late-night café. Wrapping her arms tightly around herself, she starts down the sidewalk toward it. A flicker of movement in her peripheral vision catches her eye, and her heart leaps—but it's just a sheet of newspaper blowing down the sidewalk.

Wait, *news*paper? Ana chases the paper down, grabs it out of the air, and scans the headlines:

**_Vermiletum_ Death Toll Out of Control—
Is this THE END?**

**Cover-up Suspected: How Long Has the
Government Known?**

Vaccine Rumors Prove Unfounded

It's all about the disease, every article on the whole page,
box after box, tiny print crammed across every inch of space,
like maybe the editor knew this was the last paper that would
ever be printed and wanted to fill it with everything that
needed to be said.

One article in particular catches her eye:

Vermiletum: The Germ That Destroyed the Earth

by Lauren Wong, Staff Writer

After the return of the ill-fated
APEX2 expedition survivors nearly a
year ago, it quickly became apparent
that the epidemic of death on both
APEX missions was caused by the
neurological disorder now known
as _Vermiletum._ Unofficial sources
within Savitech believe the colonists
disturbed a chemical compound
in the soil of planet Cyclid-Bf, or
Paradox; upon the APEX2 crew's
return to Earth, every adult colonist
showed signs of infection. Despite
much initial buzz on the apparent

immunity of the minors who were
part of the expedition, Savitech has
remained mum on any resulting links
or connections.

"It's a kind of mind worm," said Dr.
Rick Paolo of the Global Infectious
Disease Group (GIDG). "It anchors
itself in the brain's memory center
and then spreads outward from there
to the amygdala—the fear center of
the brain—and from there to the rest
of the body, ending in a kind of full-
body hemorrhagic attack."

No known methods of quarantine

have proven able to contain the infection. By the time it was understood that the contagion was spread by distorted brain signals, and could not be controlled by biohazard suits or disruptive barriers, the germ had spread to the public, and the cycle of death began.

While the GIDG continues to organize and moderate task forces all over the world, many experts worry that these efforts will be too late to deliver the desired results. "We are on the verge of a global epidemic," our Savitech source confirmed. "To be honest, the new mutation has us all fearing for our lives."

If our sources are to be believed, there is no longer any method of curbing the symptoms, no successful means of quarantine, and no viable hope for a cure. Dr. Paolo provided perhaps the most succinct—and chilling—analysis to date: "We have no tools to fight this. Humankind has been brought to its knees."

Ana lets go of the paper and watches it blow away down the street. Everything is eerily still. Lights are on in the buildings overlooking the street, but there are no movements inside. And there are no people, no cars—not even the sound of scurrying animals. Just the night and the wind, and the lone newspaper death-dancing down the road.

The paper catches on the bumper of a car, and Ana sees a half-empty shopping bag in the gutter next to it. Groceries are spilled across the curb. Lying next to them, half in the street, is a body. A body in a pool of blood.

She sees another body lying farther down the street, head bent at an odd angle. She turns to look behind her and sees a car—how could she have missed it?—half smashed through the window of a bank on the corner. Two or three still forms farther down the dark sidewalk look like what Ana now knows they must be: more bodies.

The dead are everywhere in this new old world.

A sob rises in her throat. Is the whole world dead?

The street is suddenly ringing with a silence that claws her ears. The thought of never hearing another voice, never seeing another person consumes her.

She yells, "Is anybody here? Is there anyone that's still alive?"

The words echo up and down the empty street. There are no survivors here. There's just the corpse of a world she cannot remember, a past she can't even properly mourn.

Though she probably won't be mourning it for long. Now that she's back, she's sure to catch this disease, too. Something that virulent? It's just a matter of time.

Then something buzzes in her back pocket.

Ana reaches down and pulls out a slim see-through device— *a phone!*—the size of her palm. She looks at the screen.

1 new text message

Her fingers tremble as she navigates the touch screen. The window opens up, and Ana falls into the words.

RU alive? Where?

A mad churning starts in Ana's stomach as she looks at the sender.

Ysa Klein

She thinks of the last time she saw Ysa on far-off Paradox, of how she was pulled out of Ana's grasp, of the fear and resignation clouding her bright eyes. Ysa is gone, Ana would swear to that.

So how is a dead girl sending her a message?

SEVENTEEN

All the way back up the elevator there's no follow-up text, no response to Ana's frantic return queries. But whether Ysa somehow survived the dunes or she came back from Paradox a zombie or this is her ghost come a-haunting, Ana cannot get up to the sixteenth floor fast enough. *Someone else is here!* She's not alone.

The elevator pings and the doors ease open.

Ana dashes down the hall to the main doors, emblazoned with the Savitech logo. She puts both hands on the door, leans against it for a second, pushing her forehead against the cool glass in a way that her body seems to remember.

For just an instant she's a younger version of herself; it's only a year or so ago, but this girl might as well be someone else entirely. This Ana bends under the weight of some invisible burden; she walks by the side of a slender light-haired boy—it's Todd—and, caught in the memory, she doesn't even have to turn her head to see the longing in his eyes when he looks at her. But this younger Ana is oblivious to it, lost in a maelstrom of internal chaos that no one else can see.

Ana lifts her head and pushes through the door, letting the memories—and her past—fall away behind her.

The room is still empty. On the television screen, one of the lights in the news studio has fallen over. It lies halfway across the newscaster's desk, glass fragments strewn every-where. Tiny blue flames lick across the papers that are scat-tered on the floor.

Ana tears her eyes away from the screen. "Ysa!" she calls. "Are you here?"

There's nothing, a nothing so thick Ana wonders if maybe she imagined the whole thing. She takes a few steps forward, and then she hears a cough and a faint, "Ana?"

It's coming from behind the door leading to the room where she woke up.

Ana passes the window showing the dark night sky, passes the worn pink couch, reaches her fingers up to the handle.

She takes a deep breath and pushes through.

The little cubicle is empty, exactly as it was when she left it.

"Ysa?" she whispers.

On the opposite side of the room, the hanging plastic strips are swaying ever so slightly.

"Ana . . ."

Ana pushes through the hanging strips and finds herself in

174

a room identical to the one she woke up in. There's another display, another tangle of machinery, another bed . . .

The world slips into syrupy slow motion as Ana wobbles toward the bed. That's not Ysa lying there. It's . . .

"Todd!" she gasps.

It's not Todd as he was on Paradox, not exactly. There's something different about his look—he seems somehow *less* than he did on the planet's rugged slopes and under its bright berry skies. His pale hair is limp and obscured by the wide black headband with its connecting web of wires and electrodes, and he has the same loose arm restraints and hip belt as she found on herself when she woke up.

But it *is* Todd.

His eyes are closed. In one hand he clutches a shiny pink phone—Ysa's phone, apparently.

"Hey," she whispers.

Todd's eyes flicker open, bright blue, so heart-wrenchingly familiar in this unfamiliar place. "You remember me," he says. His voice is scratchy but holds a note of wonder, as if she's handed him a gift he can't quite bring himself to accept.

A sob rises in her throat. "I watched you die," she says. "The worm smashed you. Back on Paradox. What happened?"

He shakes his head, a tiny motion, but she sees it. "I'm not dead . . . yet."

"How did you get back?" Ana asks. "Are you okay?"

As if in answer, Todd breaks out coughing. Ana looks at the display above his bed, which shows a series of numbers and graphs. Moving instinctively, she reaches up and touches a button on the far right side. The display changes to an ultrasound-looking readout, and Ana gasps. It's the image of a brain. *Todd's brain.*

Below the image is a line of text.

Scope of infection: 81.3%

As she watches the number shifts: 81.5%.

A bubble of blood starts in the corner of Todd's mouth, and Ana pulls the edge of the sheet up to wipe it.

"So much for our plan, huh?" Todd says.

Ana just shakes her head, trying to make sense of all the chaos inside her mind. This infection is killing everyone in the world, and now it has its grip on Todd, too.

"You don't remember anything, I know," Todd says. "I'm sorry. I wish I had"—he coughs—"told you more."

Ana takes his hand and squeezes it. "I know a little bit," she says, wishing she never had to let him go again, wishing she could will him back to health or strength or whatever he needs to fight this thing. *Can you even fight this thing?* "I know about the disease, and that everyone's dead or dying. The papers say there's no cure. Is that true? There's no hope?"

Todd smiles sadly at her. "Hope," he whispers. "That's always the starting point, isn't it? Before everything starts to go wrong. It all begins with hope. A new planet, a new world. Paradox. Where it all began."

"Paradox," she says. "We were there."

"We were," Todd agrees. "But not the way you think. Not the way you remember."

"What? I do remember it all—the Dead Forest, the rocket." She swallows. "Ysa and Chen . . ."

Todd sighs. "It really is out there, you know," he says. "Paradox, the planet. But that wasn't it. That wasn't Paradox at all." He looks right up into her eyes. "What we were in, all of that stuff you remember—that was the simulation."

"What are you talking about?"

"The sim was designed as a training device," he says. "An exact replica of the planet, reconstructed based around the specifics of the first mission, APEX1. Right down to the rockets and weapons and nasty gray jumpwear."

Ana can still feel the tearing pain in her shoulder, can hear the roar of a monster with breath as sweet as death itself, can see the twin suns, the jagged mountains, the sky and the sand and the sea.

"It wasn't real? None of that was real?"

"It *was* real," Todd says. "Just . . . inside your mind. Your body was lying in the bed in the room next to this one, while *you* were exploring Paradox. Virtually."

It's too much to take in. And yet . . . Ana rotates her shoulder again, touches her unmarked skin—no scabs, no wounds, not a single mark. She frowns as she looks at her scarred hands.

"But why—"

"We volunteered for this," Todd says. "The PX37 trials, that was the official name."

The name tickles something in her brain. Where has she heard that term?

Of course. Jackson. Bailey. PX37. The trials. Ana thinks back to Bailey's experiences: Jackson demanding results from the testing. The screened-in area where the subjects were lying. *The trials*, which were still active after everyone else was dead or dying.

What had Ana's letter said, way back at the start of it all when she first woke up in the rocket? *Your body is its own record.* She'd never imagined it would be so literally true. Her body, their bodies, in the lab. On Earth. Monitored, measured, recorded.

They were here all along.

"So we never even left Earth?" she says slowly. There's something in this thought that doesn't fit, somehow.

Todd's body shakes in a deep cough, then he says, "There's more to it than that. *This trip* was a simulation. But we did travel to the planet, the real one, over a year ago. APEX2. The second manned space mission. We were there—me and you and Chen and Ysa. You don't remember any of this, do you?"

She doesn't. But in some deep place, she knows that it's all true, everything he's saying.

Todd sighs. "Everyone was so excited for us, all the other ExtraSolar kids, the teachers—they were all jealous too, of course. They threw us the biggest send-off party. We were launching into space, real planetary travelers! But then it all went so wrong. We'd only been there a few months when mission control had us go looking for what was left of APEX1. Not that there was much to find aside from their remains . . . But shortly after that trip was when the sickness began.

"We came back, but the disease came back with us. People outside our quarantine started dying, and finally everyone realized the bug was spread by thoughts or memories, brainwaves. But the four of us, we never got sick. There were traces of the *Vermiletum* protein in our brains, but it wasn't virulent. At first they thought it had to do with us being young, but then plenty of other kids started dying. Their last theory was that it had to do with being on the planet when we were so young. Formative minds, I don't know. Somehow it protected the four of us. It couldn't help anyone else, of course."

Ana sits suddenly upright. *The four of us?* She registers the hanging plastic strips on the far side of Todd's room, identical to the ones through which she entered. "Hold on a second," she tells Todd. She puts down his hand and starts around the end of the bed.

"Wait," Todd says. "Ana!"

She pushes through the plastic strips and finds another bed, another monitor, a spaghetti-tangle of wires. And in the bed . . . at first she can't tell who it is, can't even believe there could be a person under all that *blood*. But then she notices wispy strands of yellow hair. Ysa.

She pushes through the plastic strips to the next room, eyes blurring with tears, already knowing what she will see. It's Chen, his dark spiky hair matted with blood. Ana notices a puckered burn scar covering the left side of his face. Just as her scarred hands didn't show up in what she now knows was the simulation, apparently Chen's burn mark didn't, either. And why not? If she had something to do with designing her avatar, why not create an idealized version?

Seeing Chen's scar now, Ana can't help wondering if it came about from whatever experience Chen was remembering in his final moments. *Not the fire,* he'd said. She shudders.

The display above Chen's head flashes red, the percentage readout showing 100%. Ysa's showed the same.

But something isn't making sense. Todd said that the four of them were supposed to be immune to the disease. So how is it that Chen and Ysa seem to have died of it? And something else. Ysa and Chen *died* in the simulation. Or at least . . . she thought they did.

Could it be that what *actually* killed them was the disease attacking their bodies, back here in this lab? She thinks of the way Chen slipped on what clearly was solid ground, falling into the crater. She thinks of Ysa, sucked under by sands that Todd swore were only two feet deep. Was something warped inside the simulation? Did something in there go horribly wrong?

Ana turns and pushes back through the plastic strips. She needs more answers.

EIGHTEEN

"Todd," Ana whispers, returning to his side.

Todd's eyes fly open and he sits bolt upright, circling her wrist tightly in a shaking grasp. "Just don't leave me alone in the dark, will you? That's the one thing I—" He breaks off and begins to tremble violently. Heart sinking, Ana realizes that though he's looking right at her, he's not seeing her at all. His eyes are vacant and glassy.

She glances up at his display: **83.9%**.

"Hey," she says, scooting closer, loosening his hand from hers and trying to lower him back down on the bed. But he pulls out of her grip and scoots backward. He starts twisting his head from side to side, as if scanning the room for something vitally important. "Where have you all gone? I've been in my hiding spot for ages, and nobody's found me. But now—"

Ana's heart is racing. *What can I do?*

All she can think of is the way Ysa and Chen fell into these hallucinations—*these memories*—and never came out. She leans forward and presses her face against his. "Please, Todd," she whispers. "Come back to me. Don't go like this. Please."

His body stills and then, and then—his breath catches. "Oh, Ana," he whispers, and crumples against her. "I was back there . . . I was . . ."

"Shhh," she says. "It's okay. You're okay now. It's not real."

His body is still shaking, but his eyes are clear. She props up his pillow and helps him lean back against it. A few drops of blood leak from one nostril, and Ana rubs them gently away. "It's the *Vermiletum* doing this, just like with the others," he says. "You have to keep me talking, Ana. Ask me questions. As long as I'm focusing on you and using my mind, I'm okay. It's when I'm alone that I start to drift. . . ."

"Okay," Ana says quickly. Questions, she can do. "Tell me, why did we go into the sim? What did we hope to find in there?"

"New information," Todd says. "Something, anything, we'd missed when we were actually on the planet. To help us crack the disease."

"*Experience, discover, survive,*" Ana whispers, thinking of the instructions she found in the rocket hatch. "But, Todd, it's only a simulation. What new information could we hope to learn from it?"

Todd shakes his head weakly. "The sim is more than just code. It's a real-time experience shaped moment by moment through satellite feeds and probes and the new ParSpace transmission tech. Even user memory affects the grid. It's an immersive and dynamic construction, cutting-edge stuff."

"So by going back to the source of the disease, we hoped we could uncover some type of cure?"

Todd nods. "Or something to lead us there. Anything that would help. We were supposed to follow the path we took after APEX2 landed on the planet. Submerge, gather the information, and get out. What could be simpler? Although Chen and Ysa took some persuading, they didn't want to go back, not even in the sim."

"They seemed so familiar with the planet," Ana whispers. "No wonder. They hadn't been there all along, like I thought—they had been there before, and they were back. Only . . . not back. Since it wasn't real . . ." She trails off, her mind tangling into knots, confusion still threatening to overwhelm her. "So we all made this decision to go back in, really?"

"We did. But you . . . well."

Ana looks up. "What about me?"

"You took it a step further. The simulation is rooted in the mind. It builds around existing constructs, forms around what the user already knows, inserting new and updated information as needed. You thought—what if the information we're looking for is small, or if it's something easily overlooked? What if the sim doesn't overwrite or update properly, and we miss it?"

"But if someone was a clean slate . . ."

"Right," Todd agrees, coughing and shifting in place. "If

someone went in with absolutely no baseline, a first-timer, they'd get the most accurate, up-to-date rendering of the place. The idea was for you to do the route alone, just using the map as your guide. With no preexisting expectations, you figured you would see more details, especially any *new* details."

Ana's mind is reeling. It's almost more than she can take in.

"Honestly?" Todd continues. "I think maybe you had other reasons, too, for wanting the memory wipe. That this was just part of it. But in any case, Pritchett agreed. They were so desperate they would have tried anything. Our 'trial' was a twenty-eight-hour stretch, a half cycle of what goes for daylight on the planet—Torus's sunrise to sunsmeet. Zero hour was the auto-eject. Meanwhile they could monitor our vitals and see everything we did." He closes his eyes, then opens them, looking directly into hers. "We got ready to go in, and you took the wipe. Surgical amnesia. Boom."

"Wait a minute, though," Ana says. "*You* had amnesia, too. How come you remember all this and I'm still blank? How did you get it all back?"

"No," he says, glancing quickly away. "I didn't get the wipe at all. I lied about that. I'm sorry."

"What are you talking about? Then why did you tell me you did?"

"I just . . . wanted you to feel more at ease. It seemed to make sense at the time. Then with the worm after us, it made sense to ditch the original solo plan and stick together. And once I'd started, I had to keep going with the amnesia story.

For the sake of the mission, you know, to preserve the original experiment."

Ana can tell right away that there's something he isn't telling her. But one thing's definitely true—Todd never had amnesia. And if he lied about that, what else was he faking? She has a flash of orange sunlight playing across his hair, kindling it gold and copper. She shakes her head, horrified that she can no longer even trust her own memories, sparse though they are—*it was all make-believe, all in my head . . . in more ways than one!*—and pulls herself back to the present.

Todd groans softly and Ana sees blood gathering in his left ear. Above his head, the readout shows 85.3%. His back jerks suddenly and he starts flapping his hands in front of his face. "No! Don't let it come any closer! LET ME GO!" His back arches and Ana throws herself on top of him, heart pounding, steadying his face with her hands.

"Todd," she cries, "keep fighting it. Keep talking. Come on! Tell me about the disease, Todd—the new mutation. *Vermiletum-V.* Is that what finally broke through our immunity?"

"No," Todd says weakly. He's back. For now, at least. "We went into the sim clean. We all carried the disease, of course, but it was inactive. What are you doing on top of me?"

Ana laughs shakily, rolls off, and scoots next to him on the bed. "What do you mean the disease was inactive? We were immune, then we weren't? That doesn't make any sense, unless . . . The only new variable is the simulation. Maybe there *was* something new there. Something that reversed the immunity, made us susceptible?"

Todd's nose is bleeding again, and she sees a trickle starting from his left ear. "Something was there, all right," he says. "The worm. We went and landed on Paradox after all these millions of years, digging around the worm droppings, and we set those killer spores loose and brought them back to Earth and now there's *no way to stop it!*

"Paradox." He laughs bitterly. "A fully habitable planet down to the oxygen in the air and water under the ground. Even the land formations! And then? It turns out to be not only uninhabitable but downright malignant, since it comes equipped with a mystery bug that kills everybody who sets foot there."

"So the worm is the new variable," Ana says. Her mind is working and she's suddenly seized by an urgent sense of something she might almost figure out if she tried hard enough. "Let's think about this, Todd. You said the simulation is shaped not only by satellite feed but also by our minds, right? Our memories? Okay, so *Vermiletum* lives in the brain's memory center. And going into the sim is like going directly into our own brains . . . Do you think *we* brought *Vermiletum* into the sim with us?"

Todd's eyes narrow, then widen in realization. "You mean the worm in the sim might be a physical manifestation of the disease in our minds? I don't know."

"And what about the disease itself? Think about Ysa and Chen. They shouldn't have died in that simulation. The *Vermiletum* must have been warping the land formations, messing

186

with our minds—not to mention pumping in those fear at-tacks, just like all the other victims had in the real world." *Just like you're fighting off right now,* she thinks, and her heart breaks a little more.

But Todd is nodding. "It makes sense. Somehow going into the simulation reversed our immunity and activated the dis-ease. We all caught it. Except for you." He coughs again.

"Except for me," Ana agrees. "And I think I know why: the memory wipe. Think about it: on the mountain, when the worm had us trapped in front of the cave, it ignored me, went right by me. Remember that? I thought it was chance, or lack of peripheral vision. But what if it was actually my lack of memory?"

"And when we first met, when I pulled you out of the cra-ter?" he asks.

"What if it wasn't tracking me at all that time? What if it was after you?" She shakes her head, wrings her hands together. "What if it couldn't sense me at all? Maybe being wiped actu-ally preserved my immunity!"

Todd is shaking his head. "Not for long, though. Don't you see, Ana? You started out blank, but *you can't stay that way.* You can't live without making memories."

Memories. Ana thinks about the little shreds of herself that she's gathered since first waking up from the wipe. Oddly, some of the first—and clearest, strongest—ones weren't even hers, they were Bailey's.

Oh.

The memory strands suddenly make perfect sense. While Ana's mind was connected to the sim, Bailey's disease-amplified brainwaves found her. Were they drawn to Ana in particular because of her wide-open, empty mind?

"You're right," she whispers.

Todd looks up at her so sadly. "Everything you do, every passing moment, you're forming new memories. If your theory is right, then the more time passes, the more susceptible you are."

Just then, as if to underscore his words, a cough bubbles up in Ana's chest. It's *wrong*, that cough, and when she pulls her hand away from her mouth, it's sticky with blood. Todd's right. The memory wipe didn't preserve her immunity; it just delayed it. She just took longer to develop the infection.

Frantically wiping her hand on her jeans, she glances at Todd's display monitor: 87.2%. What percentage would her own screen show if she were still connected? How far along is her infection, just now starting to show symptoms?

"I hoped . . . you would never . . ." He coughs again, his breathing rough and heavy.

"Todd," she says. She pulls her sleeve up around her hand and tries to wipe the blood from his face. There's more of it now, so much it's hard to tell where it's all coming from. She rubs at his cheeks, his eyes, knowing it's a losing battle, knowing more will just take its place.

Time freezes as Todd looks at her with those eyes that led her across Paradox, reaches up to stroke her cheek with the hand that pulled her out of the lava pit. The world is dead, she is dying, neither of them will last the day. But they have right now.

And suddenly, it's all so clear: O+O. Oslow and Ortez.

She gets it.

"Why did you let me do it?" she whispers. "Why would you let me wipe away our past?"

Todd looks confused.

"Why didn't you tell me?" she continues. "About us, I mean?"

His eyes go wide and he slowly shakes his head.

"I love you, Todd," she says. "I've always loved you. How could I ever forget that?" She leans toward him, but he lifts his hand and places it gently on her chest.

"No," he whispers.

"What do you mean, *no*?"

"No, you don't love me."

She draws back. "What are you talking about?"

"It was never like that for you. Those . . . feelings were always on my side, Ana. You saw the O+O I wrote on your letter from Pritchett? That was our joke—we were pals, business-partners-to-be, best friends, nothing more. You wiped your memory because there wasn't anything you didn't mind forgetting. You wanted me to take the wipe, too, but I couldn't let it go. Couldn't let *you* go."

Ana remembers the flash of memory she had while coming through Savitech's main doors—her younger self coming through those doors with Todd, the longing look in his eyes, and her own oblivious preoccupation. Could he be right?

Todd swallows and says, "But then we were in the sim, and

I saw the way you looked at me, as if you'd never seen me before, like I was someone special, and I thought, 'Maybe we could start again.'"

So this is what he'd been hedging about earlier, the real reason he'd pretended to have amnesia.

"But . . ." *I did,* she wants to say. *I did fall in love with you.* Except now she's confused. She *didn't* love him before? This rush of feeling, her love for Todd, has all the resonance of anything true and certain that she's learned about her past. What is she missing?

"Look," Todd says. He's trying to be light, but his words are glazed with pain. "I know things changed for you after the wipe. But think about the circumstances: Alien planet, constant danger, on the run from a rampaging beast. Of course you liked me. Hey," he says, and tries for a grin, but his life's spilling out before her eyes. "I'm a charming guy."

Ana shakes her head. So she really didn't love him. Then again, should it even matter? How much of a connection is there between the person she was and the person she is now? As much connection as there is between real life and the simulation? Ana grows suddenly still. There's a thread here, something tugging at her, and abruptly she shifts mental paths in order to follow it.

She rewinds to the beginning of what she knows: Somehow, entering the simulation activated *Vermiletum* for her, Todd, Ysa, and Chen, shifting the infection from dormant to virulent. Meanwhile, scientists and researchers around the world had been unable to find a way to affect *Vermiletum. In the real world.* But inside the simulation, the *Vermiletum* took on a body, the form of the worm.

And something that has a body can be killed.

What if . . . what if she could kill the worm in the sim? Would that be the same as cleansing the disease from her brain?

And then, beyond that—she can't allow herself to think, to hope, but the words from Bailey's report sweep through her head, that a reversal of the disease in *just one person* might start a cascade effect. Could curing one person of the disease really provoke a reverse infection that would sweep out to others, too?

"Ana," Todd whispers. His eyes are starting to glass over, his mouth opens, and she can see the effort it takes for him to pull back, to return to her.

She looks up at his readout: **93.7%**.

"Todd," she says. She leans forward and places her lips on his, whisper-kissing her breath into his mouth. "There's something I need to do. Can you hold on a little longer? For me?"

"You," he says, gasping, "are the past and the future. You are all there is. You will always . . . own me."

How can she leave him like this, knowing where the disease is going to take him? But she also knows that her presence alone won't be enough to save him. Not for long. His only hope—*their* only hope—lies in this step she's about to take.

She has to try.

"Todd." She cups a hand on either side of his head and looks into his face.

His eyes are growing dull and his lips form soundless words, but his hand moves up toward her. She feels his cold touch on her face, drawing a circle on her right cheek, then one on her left. He shifts down to her chin and draws a line up and then across.

O+O

The world is a snow globe and she is trapped inside, trapped here next to the only thing that matters, maybe the only thing that ever mattered, and still—*still*—not able to remember him. What kind of person scrubs her whole past out of her mind? What could possibly justify it?

Is the past a worthwhile exchange for the future?

And meanwhile, Todd is trapped in his past and he's dying. He's *dying!* If she can do anything to save him, she can't do it from here.

Ana rests Todd's arms gently by his sides, then turns and walks back to her own little room.

It's not just Todd who's dying—she is, too. There's one last hope, one chance. It's that paradox all over again. They went into the simulation to find a cure to the disease, and ended up finding a quicker way to die. Well, now she intends to do everything she can to bring about a death. Maybe through it, someone somewhere will have a shot at life.

She's going back to Paradox.

Part 3

NINETEEN

Ana comes awake underwater. There is pressure on her chest and a roaring in her ears. She opens her eyes and everything is a deep, murky green.

Apparently she did a lousy job modifying the simulator's coordinates; she didn't want to start off back at the rocket, but she didn't want to drown, either!

Thick and viscous, the dark green water clings to her like a heavy blanket. She's back in her jumpsuit and vest—no backpack, thank goodness—and her boots are two anchors dragging her down. Pulling her knees to her chest, she rips at the laces. Her lungs are screaming. She kicks off both of her boots, her socks sliding easily in their wake, and pulls toward the light.

She breaks the surface and gulps in a deep breath of clean air. Now supported by the same dense water that was dragging her down a moment ago, Ana churns her feet gently and paddles her hands, moving in a full circle. She's quite far out to sea—the shore is maybe a half mile away, pale and sandy. Down the coast she can just make out the broken-down stone walls of the old APEX base.

Overhead, the sky is afire. Torus is a blazing bowling ball toppling into the far horizon, so bright and so close to the edge of the world, with the rim of the sun stretching out tendrils toward the land as if it can't wait to go play in the shadows. High overhead, Anum holds its place, but it looks pale and washed out by comparison with its fiery twin. This view of the world looks beautiful, but ominous, too; heavy with the promise of shadows to come.

Ana set the simulation's auto-eject for two hours, so she has that long—assuming she doesn't succumb to the infection before then—to find the worm and destroy it. How things go forward from there, she has no way of knowing for sure. But if there's even a chance of success, she has to try. For Todd, for herself—the Ana she once was, the one she killed inside her own mind—and for any other survivors who might be just holding on, or who might be isolated somewhere and still uninfected.

There is no one else. It's up to her.

She's almost turned a full circle when she sees a whirlpool forming ahead of her. It churns faster and faster until the worm erupts into the air with a roar, bald head glistening, sleek and almost graceful on water like it never was on land.

There's no need to find the worm; the worm has found her.

Out here on the open sea, there is no grinding noise, but the worm is far from silent. Ana's blood chills at the screech of metal and the eerie tinkle of smashing glass that echoes inside her head. She had suspected that these sounds were linked to the fear memories—just like Todd's ordeal in the forest, Chen's fire, and Ysa's attack under the bleachers—and everything she's read about *Vermiletum* has confirmed that to be true. These noises must be the link to whatever nightmare memory the disease is trying to drag back into her own mind as it hammers at her body with the infection. It's the sound track to her own worst memory. A memory she doesn't even have—yet still, she can feel the infection pushing at the edge of her mind, trying to find a way in: first memory, then fear, then paralysis and mania.

She pushes back. It's all she can do.

The worm dives underwater and disappears. For one heart-beat, the world is frozen. Then the worm is back, rising out of the depths just in front of Ana with a bellowing roar and a cascade of churning, foaming white water.

In desperation, Ana takes a breath and slides below the surface.

She dives deep and finds herself below the worm's vast body. It looks like a brown wall rippling through curtains of stringy seaweed. It's so big! How did she think she was going to kill this thing? The pistol has to be useless after this kind of a soaking. So it's down to her two knives—next to nothing against a beast this size.

But that doesn't change a thing. She's here and she's alive. As long as there's breath in her body, her real body, back in the Savitech lab on the decimated Earth, she's going to fight this monster.

Watching the worm pass, Ana begins to formulate a plan. Todd tried attacking it head-on; it didn't work. Climbing over the worm's face is way too risky. But attacking from behind . . .

She pulls toward the worm's leathery flank, but before she can grab ahold of it, the tail whips by as the worm breaches again. There's a muffled splash as it reenters the water behind her and disappears.

She's missed her chance.

Ana kicks out and propels herself upward. She breaks the surface—*for one horrible second like crashing through a pane of glass, hands first, searing pain*—and then she's treading water again, surrounded by a dark sea and a purpling sky.

Was that her own memory trying to break through? She can only hope her memory wipe will protect her long enough to accomplish what she needs to do.

But the worm . . . where did it go?

With a gurgling splash it's back, the worm's head and body erupting from the water behind her in a fountain of cascading water and algae. Ana pulls her body through the waves, fighting her logical mind and swimming toward the beast's flank instead of away from it. She closes the distance and throws out her hands. The worm's hide looks leathery but it's rough, as hard as iron, and pockmarked with little holes and craters.

Gritting her teeth, Ana wedges one hand into a crevice, and hangs on. In an instant, she's airborne and scrabbling with her free hand and with her feet, trying to find other holds. She finds them just in time, clinging tightly to the worm's side as it reaches the top of its jump, then turns and crashes back into the water. She takes a deep breath and holds on as the worm dives down—down—down. The water turns from green to mud to coal black. Ana squeezes her eyes shut and concentrates on keeping her fingers and toes wedged into the worm's hide.

Then the worm is climbing again. They break the surface, and Ana begins moving. Slowly and laboriously, she starts to scale the flank of the giant worm as it swims along the surface of the sea. It takes just a few minutes to get to the top of the creature's back, minutes that feel like hours, but finally she's there. She positions herself in the center of the worm's back.

The worm makes a sharp turn and she is thrown backward and she's slipping, skidding down the worm's back, scrabbling for handholds as the bony ridge along the worm's back tears down the front of her body. Her bare feet scrape along the worm's scaly outer shell.

The ridge is clawing up her middle, but it's also her salvation. She throws her weight into her hands and forces them to close around the protrusion. Her fingers wedge into place and she skids to a stop.

Now the worm settles into a smooth forward pace. Instead of diving, it begins to dip shallowly through the water and then flatten out, swimming along the surface, undulating easily like a snake. Ana lifts her head and squints into the fine spray circling the worm's body. The worm seems to be swimming for shore. There's a beach ahead, though she can no longer see any sign of the APEX compound. In fact, she can see lots of trees, green trees, and wonders whether this is even the same shore.

Time is running out—she has to get to the worm's head.

The worm's body is divided into segments, each one almost twice the length of her own body. The plates slip and slide and overlap each other as the worm shimmies its way across the sea.

Now, the time is now, she thinks as she slides her right foot forward. Immediately, she feels a searing pain. She screams and looks back.

Her foot has slid onto the overlap between two sections. The area is sticky and gooey, even with the seawater cascading down the worm's back. Fluid oozes out from between the overlapping plates in the worm's armor, and it's coated her foot.

She yanks her foot out of the crack but it's too late. The pain is like white-hot blades of fire. She can barely stand to move it.

At the same time, she feels again the push of broken glass trying to force its way into her mind. For a second it's almost as if the worm itself is inside her head, looking into her soul.

Of course, the worm *is* in her head. *She* is in her head.

Nothing about this showdown is physically real. And yet it's the only way to save her life—and maybe, also, the world.

The worm's body jerks and Ana slides forward, her good foot scrabbling against the worm's armor.

Ana glances at her circlet; her two hours are nearly half gone. She looks up. The sky is a hard cranberry and edging fast toward plum. Torus is nothing but a glowing half circle on the far horizon. The land is near and getting nearer, and the worm's travel is steady enough that Ana thinks she might be able to stand and walk along its back. If her damaged foot will let her.

I can do this, she thinks, willing the words to be true.

Ana slides her hands to her chest, then scoots her left foot forward so that she's crouching. Her right foot is tougher to position. It's covered in red welts and ridges, and the fluid from the worm's joint glows a pale luminescent green. She wobbles as the worm angles to the left, but manages to keep her balance. The pain in her foot hasn't let up, though at least it hasn't moved any farther up her leg. But her foot is as numb as a sock filled with sand, and when she tries to put weight on it, she pitches forward.

She catches herself on her hands and gasps when she sees how close she's landed to the next seam. The thick goo glows eerily in the gathering dusk, seeping and trickling from the crack.

It's easier to get moving the second time. She slides her injured foot along without really lifting it—scoot, step, slide—keeping her stance wide and her hands thrust out to the side.

She crosses three segments this way. Overhead the sky is

a giant purple bruise over the land. Anum glows pale and in-
effective in the darkening sky; Torus is nearly fully set. She's
almost there. She thinks again of Todd's wide, staring eyes, his
last heartbreaking smile. She can't lose him. She *can't.*

Ana's whole foot is throbbing, like dozens of tiny teeth
chewing the end of her nerves, but she's only three seams
away from the head. She has to do this. She's so close.

The worm is stretched out flat on the water now, and Ana
can feel the wind whistling past her ears. She looks up ahead—
and then the worm hits the beach, hits it like a batter sliding
into third, arcing out of the water and grinding up the shore
in a cresting wave of sand.

The force of the landing sends Ana flying off her position
on the worm. She hurtles through the air and hits the sand,
landing hard on her back. For a second the air is knocked out
of her lungs and she feels something in her chest go *crunch.* A
rib?

Tears fill her eyes as she scrambles to her feet, reaches
down, and draws her long blade out of its sheath on her hip.
The worm is just across the sand, its head high in the air and
scanning the landscape . . . but looking in the opposite direction. It's looking away from her, toward a gaping hole in the
ground. A burrow? Is this its nest? Its original resting place,
back on the Paradox of so long ago?

Limping, Ana starts toward the creature. The plan hasn't
changed—get on its back, climb to the head, and stick her
dagger as deep as she can between its eyes.

She doesn't take three steps before her foot twists under her and she falls flat on her face in a cloud of sand. She lets out a low moan. How can she climb onto the worm's back with her foot like this?

The worm's still facing away from her, but its tail now twists in her direction.

She gets shakily to her feet, casting a desperate look around her. In the rapidly dimming light, she sees lumpy forms along the shore. Long, spindly shapes, all stick-bones and torsos . . .

Skeletons, bleached human bones, and grinning skulls, a half dozen or more, lying strewn all around her.

What is this place?

While she's looking at the bones, the worm's long body loops slowly, so slowly around, until she is fully trapped. Only then, *only then* does the worm's head start to turn in her direction.

And now the familiar grinding noise starts up again, with its new accents of crunching metal and shattering glass. It's loud, bone-jarringly loud as it courses through her body and the beach and the sand and everything is shaking like an earthquake and the worm rears and with it the pressure on her mind, *in* her mind, increases like the worm is physically trying to get in, as if it's trying to force back in the memory that will anchor her to the disease.

She'd wanted to face down the worm, but not like this.

The front portion of the worm's body crunches across the sand toward her, while its tail segments stay in place, blocking her escape. The creature's bottomless eyes are like polished black glass, and suddenly they ripple like mirrors, like memory. *No! I have no memories!* And the noise is getting louder, the crush and grind and break of metal and glass like jagged shards digging into her, biting hot and sharp, trying to claw something loose inside her head.

The worm rises slowly to tower over her.

Its jaw opens wide, a circle like the night sky itself pulsing above her, like something as big as her entire world, something too big to outrun.

But she's not running.

"I'm not going anywhere," Ana whispers as Torus's last bright edge slides under the far horizon, plunging the world into shadow. She whips out her dagger and shifts her feet into a fighting stance.

Its maw still gaping wide, the worm dives.

TWENTY

A gust of hot, sweet air rushes down to meet Ana as she leaps up and off her good foot, blade outthrust.

She lashes out wildly with the dagger and plunges it into something coarse and gluey. Ana finds herself suspended in midair, hanging from her dagger in complete darkness. She can't see a thing around her. Then there's a jolt, and she starts to move. *Oh.* She's inside the worm's mouth. It went down and she went up and—

She must have jumped right past the rows of razor teeth.

The worm swallowed her whole.

Ana swings her feet around, looking for purchase, but her hands are supporting all of her weight, and her fingers are slick with sweat. It's getting harder and harder to hold on. The worm lurches, and Ana loses her grip on the dagger's hilt. Her blade still caught in the worm's side, she tumbles down to land onto a gummy, mushy surface.

Fumbling in the dark, Ana activates the map on her circlet and shines the light around. She's in a damp, cavernous space that curves up to a peaked, bony ridge above her head. The walls are fleshy and dripping with fluid, which pools in a shallow stream around her feet.

She feels a prickling in her uninjured foot and gasps in realization: That neon ooze between the segments wasn't acid. It was . . . digestive juice? Her left foot is raw in the dim half-light. Even worse, her jumpsuit is soaked with it; she can feel a burning sensation starting up all over her body. How long can she last in here before she's broken down for food?

She hears and feels the worm grind into motion, crushing across the sand outside, and again her head resounds with the screeching of tearing metal and the crash of shattering glass.

There's another sharp stab in her mind, and she knows what's coming and she tries to fight it off but she can't, not this time. It's right in the middle of her head, pain like nothing she's ever felt before, pain and heat and flashing lights and movement, faster and faster—

She's at the wheel and she's angry, steaming with the pent-up rage that comes from a lifetime of maintaining control.

"No," Mom says. "You're not going and that's final. If I had known that's where this was heading, I never would have let you sign up for that program."

"You didn't let me sign up, Mom. They recruited me in spite of you."

There's a driving rain pelting the windshield outside, but that's not what's making her eyes blurry. Ana clenches the steering wheel more tightly.

"Look, I'm sorry I never told you more about your dad," Mom says. "I know that's what this is all about. It's just . . . it's all still so painful."

Caught off guard by the softer tone, Ana glances over, just in time to catch sight of the tear rolling down her mother's cheek. Her graying hair's come loose from its severe bun and she's tucking and smoothing frantically, like even now she's working to fix things, to make everything look okay.

"Look, Mom," Ana says, "I don't want to upset you, but you've got to understand. Those Savitech registration forms you signed last year leave all the final decision making to me. You can't stop me from going."

"It's not safe," Mom whispers. "Something's not right on that planet. I can't lose you, too."

Ana groans. "You're not going to lose me! It's the expedition of a lifetime—we're going to be heroes. We'll go down in history!"

"That's what we said, too." She sighs. "Do you know what your dad's last words to me were?"

A tremor starts deep in Ana's chest. At last she's going to find out what happened to take her father away from her before she was born. Maybe if she knows that, she won't need to escape across the galaxy, just as long as she can find out what really happened, just as long as she can know.

And then—

The world flips over.

The steering wheel slips and it's only for a second that everything gets away from her but then it's all too fast and oh God that was a corner but the car's not turning not turning not turning and there's a hand on her arm, her mother's hand grabbing her and her mouth forming words that she can't make out because there's a light shining in her eyes there is noise and the *loudest sound she's ever heard filling her ears, metal tearing, ripping apart like tissue paper, and blood and fear and heat and the whole world exploding and her hands are flying forward bursting through burning glass and everything is sharp, white-hot pain—*

Ana topples forward on her hands and knees.

The worm's flesh under her is soft and it's burning into her hands, but she doesn't care. As they sear and blister in the worm's acid, she can see them twisting into the shape of her real-life hands—scar for scar, burn for burn, slice for slice— those hands that punched through the windshield in the fatal accident that *she* caused.

The accident, she now knows, that only she survived.

She understands now why she would exchange the memories of a lifetime for the chance to start over. The blame and guilt and crippling grief fall on her in a devouring swell, and even though she knows the worm is using those feelings to push deeper into her mind, she can't muster the strength or even the will to push them away.

She wants to weep. Chen's and Ysa's deaths—the versions she witnessed, anyway, here on Paradox—take on new meaning for her, the way the warping of their bodies echoed what was going on in their minds. No wonder Chen took that last fateful step into the crater—*not giving up*, he said, *just letting go*—surrendering to the disease in the face of an unrelenting loop of his most terrifying memory. And Ysa, literally drowning in fear. And Todd . . .

Oh, Todd! Is this what you are feeling, too?

She sees his face as she last saw it, eyes smiling though his lips could barely move. She feels his finger tracing the lines of her face. And then she knows—she knows—

He wasn't letting go of anything.

And if Todd is fighting so hard to hold on, how can she give up? With all the world hanging in the balance, in the end it's just for one person that she will get up and keep going.

She has to try again.

———

TWENTY-ONE

Regrouping for another attack is easier said than done. Ana drags herself to her feet and, as best as she can, wipes the worm's digestive juice off of her hands and on her pants. Her hands are red and swollen and covered in blistering sores, but she can still use them. The pain is good; it grounds her to what is real.

As real as this world gets, anyway.

But what can she do with those damaged hands? Her pistol is waterlogged and useless, the knife too small to do much against the worm, and her dagger is stuck above her head, in the roof of the worm's mouth.

Wait. In the worm's *mouth?*

Ana swings the light from her circlet around until she sees the hilt above and in front of her, behind the last row of the worm's jagged teeth. Staggering, she reaches out to clutch the fleshy wall of the worm's throat. It feels like a giant wet sponge, but it's easy enough to wedge her fingers into the mushy stuff to help her walk.

She stumbles forward, moving toward the worm's teeth until she's standing just below the dagger—looking impossibly, unreachably high. The worm's inner wall is softer here, it's like trying to grab a feather pillow. Her hand sinks in past her wrist, but she grips the flesh firmly and gets ready. Digging in her toes, with a hunk of flesh in each hand, Ana climbs.

About halfway up the wall, she thinks she feels a tremor under her hands and feet. Was that her imagination, or did the worm's body twitch? Can it feel this?

The climb seems to take forever, though it can't be more than several minutes before Ana reaches the dagger. She's hanging nearly upside down from the roof of the creature's mouth. The last thing she wants to do is fall again, so she digs her feet and one of her hands in as deep as she can before she reaches over to slowly and methodically pry the dagger loose. Yes!

What now?

The dagger had been wedged into the underside of the long bony ridge that runs the length of the worm's body. The ridge starts just behind that last row of teeth. If the worm's anatomy is laid out in a logical manner, Ana's willing to bet that its brain is somewhere just above that point. With any luck, the roof of its mouth will be soft enough for her to saw through and reach that vital organ.

Or something, anything, that will make an impact.

At this point, she can't afford to be picky.

She'll need both her hands for this next step. She puts the blade between her teeth and bites down on it hard, nearly gagging at the foul worm-slime that covers it. Still mostly upside-down, she inches her way across the roof of the worm's mouth, her arms screaming and every movement sending jolts of pain through her damaged rib.

Hand over fist, foot over leg. It's painfully slow going.

And still she can feel the worm beating at the edges of her mind, trying to find purchase and get back in. That one-time memory wasn't enough; the disease won't stop until she is stuck in an endless replay loop of that moment, over and over. Until she's dead.

She keeps moving, struggling to hold on, though she doesn't think she can last much longer.

Finally, she's there.

X marks the spot, she thinks.

Gripping the dagger in her left hand, she thrusts upward with all her might.

The knife easily slices into and through the worm's flesh— until it doesn't. Halfway in, the blade stops with a dull *thunk* and goes no farther. The force of the aborted blow is jarring, and Ana's numb toes slip.

She falls, screaming in frustration, trying and failing to hold on, grabbing at the dagger, which comes loose and arcs down with her. She lands with a splash of digestive juices, the knife spiraling away down the worm's throat.

No!

The worm's body twists and turns, tossing Ana from side to side. Her blow didn't break through, but the monster must have felt it. Ana can sense the pressure in her head mounting—*there's rain and the steering wheel is blistering hot in her hands and the wind whips the car to the side, and—*

Ana screams again. She has to stay in control! She has to kill the worm.

But what can she do against it now? She's weaponless, and the worm is burrowing deeper. It's in her head, in her mind, and . . . *Wait.*

Just like real life to the sim, and then the sim to real life. The worm is in her mind. . . .

And if it works one way, why not the other?

It's such a risk, such a terrible risk. She's not even sure she has the strength to accomplish what she suddenly understands is needed. But if she fights the creature face to face, there is absolutely no way she can win.

It's this shot or nothing.

Ana takes a deep breath and opens herself to the memory—*tears pouring down her mother's face*—embraces it—*tears like the rain, like blood*—welcomes it—*wind lashing the car*—accepts it—*the lurch and spin, the loss of control*—accepts herself.

Suddenly Ana discovers she is less *in* the memory and more to the side of it, watching, free of the devastating emotional riptide. She lets it rush around her, watches again as her younger self loses control on that dark windswept night, watches as everything she has left in the world is torn away from her, and then—*blood and twisting metal and the screeching of brakes and everywhere the horrible smell of burning*—Ana pulls the memory tight inside her mind for one trembling moment, catches her breath—

And then flings it outward.

The car explodes, shattering the air around her and filling the worm's body with razor-sharp glass and white-hot metal and horrible, crunching death. Thick liquid pours over her broken body, covering her face, running down her neck as the beast roars and roars and roars.

Ana knows she's in the simulation, knows with every part of her that it's not real it's still not real none of this is happening, but the pressure is still clawing, raging in her head, and she knows it's the worm fighting for its life now, but if it's fighting then it must be dying—it *is* dying, she knows that, she can feel it inside her brain, clawing on to life, trying to inflict as much damage as it can, but—

It's weakening.

As she holds on, the pulses of pain grow fainter and the grinding grows quiet. There is a dull, reality-shaking *boom* and a rush of cold air, and Ana falls to the ground, the hard-packed, blood-soaked sand of Paradox beach.

Ana is alone in the dim half-light, and there's not a breath, not a movement, not a sound.

The worm is dead.

She closes her eyes.

TWENTY-TWO

When Ana opens her eyes, the light around her is clean and white, and the air is still. There's no wind, no waves, no sand in her hair or grit in her teeth.

She sits up slowly, trying to reorient her mind. The two hours have expired; she's back in her little room at Savitech. First things first: she turns to check the monitor behind her. The panel is flashing bright green:

Infection: 0%

Some wall inside her mind bursts, the dam behind which she had held back her hopes, her fears, all the ways that it couldn't be possible, that it could never work. And yet—it has! She's done it. Somehow she turned the tables, took the worm's own weapon and used it against the creature. And won! Killing the worm in the simulation has cleared the malignancy from her brain as well.

And if the virus is connected the way the researchers thought, the way she hopes . . .

She swallows a sob, only wishing that she could have learned this, *done this*, sooner.

Working quickly, she disconnects herself from the simulation's wiring, then slides off the bed, pushes through the plastic strips, and steps into the adjoining room. Todd is lying where she'd left him, his face covered with dark red blood. Is he breathing?

One of his hands is stretched slightly out, index finger pointing toward the door.

Ana's heart skips a beat.

Before she left, she'd laid his arms flat by his side. He wasn't gone yet then, so *there's still hope!* Dropping to her knees by his bedside, she holds his wrist to check for a pulse, laying her ear on his chest . . . but she can't tell. She's so nervous she can't tell anything right now.

She looks at the display monitor.

Infection: 99%

Ana's heart sinks, crashes right down onto the rocks and shatters into a million fragments. But wait . . . 99% isn't 100%. She thinks of the readouts over Chen's and Ysa's beds. *That's* what final looked like. There's still time.

There's still hope.

But what can she do? She thinks again about Bailey's report. She's cleared the disease from her own mind—that's the first step. Now she just has to give it time and hope that science is on her side, that the infection *did* permanently change her brain—and that it changed again with the worm's death—so it will still be transmitting signals, yes, but not one that's radiating out the disease.

Now, she hopes, her brain is transmitting a signal that will do just the opposite.

Ana leans over and rests her head on Todd's shoulder, letting herself remember him. She remembers his hand reaching over the cliff's edge, pulling her up to safety. She remembers the look he gave her, as if he saw who she really was, someone she herself didn't even know. She remembers his voice in the cave, soothing her to sleep. And as all these memories flood through her, a feeling surges inside her, a feeling that goes right to her core. And suddenly she knows that she fell in love with Todd Oslow on Paradox—simulation or not—because she *was* in love with him before. She's been in love with him all along.

Maybe she wouldn't acknowledge it then, buried as she was under the crushing weight of her own guilt and pain— maybe she didn't even fully know how she felt. But that love was there, below the surface. And it wouldn't be kept away.

Ana closes her eyes and lets the tears come. She's lost so much of herself, her past, but this one thing, so late—too late—has come back to her.

She's so lost in thought that the faint *ping* from above her doesn't register at first. But when it does, her heart leaps into her throat and her eyes fly to the display.

Infection: 93%

Ana's eyes widen as she watches the number quickly fall: 89% . . . 85% . . .

Todd's breathing is labored and slow, but she can hear it clearly now: 79%. His eyes flicker open for one quick second, then drift shut again. And Ana knows—knows in the deepest part of her—that he *will* recover. It will be a slow process, she's sure. But he's going to make it: 67%.

And if Todd can make it, then why not others? There must be people still alive, people who are not yet infected, or who contracted the infection late and haven't yet succumbed.

55%

She has no idea what happens next.

But if there are survivors to be found, she will find them. She and Todd together. There's still so much that's broken inside her, but her new foundation is strong and clean and ready to work. After all, there's a lot broken about this new world, too:

Ana knows that it's nothing she can't handle.

She's going forward.

APPENDIX A

Interview with Rosa Ortez, APEX1

Savitech Corporation (Office #3476):
Boston, Massachusetts, September 2041

CONFIDENTIAL—Internal Eyes Only!

Q: Please state your name, age, and occupation for the record.

R/O: My name is Rosa Ortez. I am thirty-nine years old. I am an astrophysicist employed by Savitech. Or I was.

Q: Please explain how you came to be part of APEX1.

R/O: I've been working in astrophysics for seventeen years. I was recruited by Savitech out of MIT and completed my doctorate at Princeton with a special focus on manned spaceflight and the greater physical solar system. I met Jim there. . . . We were colleagues. . . .

Q: How did you come to be part of APEX1?

R/O: When the trip was planned, Jim and I both knew we wanted to be on it. Savitech was heavily involved in the mission from the start, a big sponsor, so we were right in the loop. The day we learned we were going to be part of the team to Paradox was the happiest of our lives. If only we'd known then . . .

Q: How did you come to be carrying a child on the eve of such an important and far-reaching mission into space?

R/O: That was never supposed to happen. Jim and I had no plans to have children, and we certainly weren't trying for it at the time. I don't know what went wrong. We went into partial suspension for the flight. By the time we woke up months later on Paradox, it was plainly visible.

Q: What happened next?

R/O: Jim was frantic, as you might imagine. He wanted me to return to Earth immediately, but how could I do that? The ships carry four, and the idea of either taking half the team back with me or leaving them stranded was unthinkable. Jim insisted that at least I shouldn't go on the early scouting trips, not until they knew everything on the planet was safe.

Q: What scouting trips were these?

R/O: The early exploratory sweeps, checking out the landscape. The Cranium was a perfect landing zone, but it was no place to set up a permanent colony. The planet has a huge groundwater lake, the Maraqa Sea, and that's where we were going to establish the colony, somewhere along the shore.

Q: So you stayed with the rocket.

R/O: That's right. I was close to four months pregnant, after all. Jim and the others set off. They had their communicators, and they kept in touch.

Q: How did you occupy yourself during this time?

R/O: They had gone out in a few different directions, and I spoke with each team two or three times a day, plotting their course and keeping notes on their findings. I also started taking soil samples and logging plant life. . . .

Q: When did you first suspect that something had gone wrong?

R/O: It happened so suddenly. It was two weeks after the landing, and they had found a spot that looked promising. Everyone had gathered as a group in that location to do some digging—excavating on the shore in preparation for setting up a base. I was getting ready to make the trip over to join them—Jim was going to come back and escort me in a few days. And then . . .

Q: Yes?

R/O: And then . . . things got weird.

Q: Ms. Ortez?

R/O: (crying) The communicators kept turning off and on, like there was some kind of interference. But . . . I'm sorry, no matter how many times I go over it in my mind, it still doesn't make any sense.

Q: Just state the facts, Ms. Ortez.

R/O: I heard Jim yelling. It was like he was seeing something. Almost like one of those really bad nightmares, where you're reliving something horrible from your past. He kept yelling about an ambush. He was in the war years ago, but . . .

Q: (clears throat)

R/O: I heard gunfire—everyone was carrying the standard-issue weapons. Then I lost contact for a while.

Q: How did you discover what happened to them?

R/O: They had left the remo-bot with me, the little robot-camera on wheels. I sent off the bot, and I waited, all the while scanning the channels, trying to pick up any more communications. There was nothing. The bot took hours to get there. But when it finally did . . .

Q: What did the robot show you, Ms. Ortez?

R/O: They were all dead. Jim was holding his pistol; they all were.

Q: Captain James Ortez murdered his companions.

R/O: No! That's not what happened. You have to believe me!

Q: We've been over this many times, Ms. Ortez. Will you describe the scene exactly as you saw it?

R/O: Jim's pistol was in his hand. He'd been shot in the side of the head. The others . . . The others were all turned away, like they'd been trying to run. They'd been shot in the back. I know what you're thinking, but I know Jim. There's no way he shot them.

Q: Despite the fact that he left his wife in safety before doing so?

R/O: I was pregnant! Why is everybody focusing on the wrong things? What about the strange stuff he was yelling about? That's on the tapes! Why are you talking to me instead of analyzing that? And I told you they'd been digging. They'd uncovered something . . . I couldn't tell from the feed, but it looked like some kind of huge hole, like a tunnel or cave. It was right on the shore of the sea. The sides of the hole were ridged, like it was a burrow for some kind of enormous creature.

Q: Ms. Ortez, you conducted life-sweep testing, did you not?

R/O: The tests showed no living creatures on the planet. But maybe—

Q: I think we are nearly finished here. What did you do next?

R/O: What could I do next? What was there to do? Jim was gone. They were all gone. The ParSpace communicator back to Earth never worked . . . what a joke that was. The only thing I could do was come back home. I sealed the hatches and powered the engines. I got back twenty-three days ago, just in time to go into labor. If my child had died from all she had to go through in transit, I wouldn't have been surprised.

Q: She did not die.

R/O: No. In fact, I need to go and feed her now. She's all I have left, you see? I've told you everything, and not for the first time. May I go now?

Q: Yes. We appreciate your time, Ms. Ortez. I would like to inform you officially that the board is fully satisfied that you had no part in this tragedy. And that in deference to his years of service and contribution to the space-travel initiative, details of Captain Ortez's demise will not be made public. You have been through a great deal, and Savitech is grateful for your service.

R/O: You think you're being generous, don't you? The only good thing that came from this experience is my precious girl. My little one. My Ana.

APPENDIX B

APEX2 TRANSMISSIONS LOG

PARSPACE8 DEDICATED CHANNEL 4057.3

Encoded Transmission 12182057-000BX

<Test signal sent from launchpad.
All systems prepared for departure
at 0600 tomorrow morning. Beginning
pre-suspension sequence. Future
transmissions will come from space.
Hoorah!>

Encoded Transmission 04012058-008XR

<APEX2 has landed! Repeat: We have set
foot on Paradox. Journey smooth, no
obstacles. Suspended animation reverse
activate a complete success. All sixteen
colonists accounted for. Eager to
begin exploration. We set out at dawn
tomorrow. You would not believe the sky
on this planet!>

Encoded Transmission 04282058-021RI

<Initial scouting parties settled on
an optimal spot to establish colony:
along the south shore of Maraqa Sea.
What a view you Earthlings are missing!
Water brackish and unusually thick but
potable. Some edible native plant life.
No detectable animal life forms.>

Encoded Transmission 06092058-032BX

<Construction continues at rapid pace.
External walls up and temporary shelters
fully begun. All hands healthy and hard
at work. This is a wonderful new land!>

Encoded Transmission 06212058-039BX

<In reply to query: No sign of APEX1
location. Will investigate at first
opportunity, but weather is growing
colder and shelters must be complete
before turning attention to other
pursuits.>

Encoded Transmission 08302058-061BX

<This land needs more settlers!
Temporary shelters are up and in use.
Begin investigation into APEX1 fate on
the morrow. Huzzah for Paradox!>

Encoded Transmission 10112058-121BX

<Inclement weather delayed APEX1
investigation process somewhat. Teams
have now traveled to west and east. Work
on permanent housing facilities also
begun. Will report on further results
going forward.>

Encoded Transmission 11082058-153BX

<Inconsistent feedback from team
exploring far north along Maraqa coast.
Results unclear. More news forthcoming.>

Encoded Transmission 11112058-159BX

<APEX1 site location confirmed. Seven
bodies, fully decomposed, forensic
evidence at the site consistent with

footage and prior reports received.
Strange illness overtaken three of five
colonists returned from site.>

Encoded Transmission 12192058-199BX

<Have sustained fatality. Unknown
illness appears to cause brain fever
and paranoid hallucinations, with a
subsequent spread to attack internal
functions. Please advise.>

Encoded Transmission 12272058-217BX

<Three more fatalities. This is reaching
epidemic proportions. Suggested control
measures not working. Have isolated
eleven remaining healthy persons within
the rockets. Please advise.>

Encoded Transmission 01102059-234BX

<Do not agree with proposed plan of
action. Must return survivors to safety.
Two more within the colony have died.
Launching suspended animation and return
travel sequence within 48 hours. Confirm
launch coordinates that follow.>

APPENDIX C

Prepared Statement Delivered December 14, 2057,
by Ana Ortez, Austin Space Launch Facility

Ladies and gentlemen, on the eve of going into seclusion to prepare for the APEX2 launch next week, I have been asked to deliver a statement on behalf of the ExtraSolar Youth Science team. We're immensely proud to have been chosen to represent Earth on this mission. We might be young, but we've been preparing for this journey our whole lives. We will not let you down!

Humankind is on the verge of something so enormous, most of us can't even begin to imagine the repercussions. But I'm here to tell you that there's nothing to worry about and everything to look forward to. As my mother used to say, there's more than one way to season the soup, and I think we've hit on the best one. We are venturing into the darkest reaches of space with just one goal: to meet this planet, to embrace it, to receive what it has to offer. And to use what we learn there to shape the world we live in now. This is our dream. This is our hope. This is our future.

One year from now, what brave new world will we be a part of? Only time will tell. All I know for sure is this: The next time we speak I will be lifting my glass to you in a toast at the end of the universe.

To the future!

ACKNOWLEDGMENTS

Every book begins as an idea, and this one is no exception. The process whereby that idea—in this case, a character who grabbed my imagination by the throat and would not let go—grows slowly into something resembling a finished product is one that I could never undertake alone. To those many of you who helped me along the way, my deepest thanks.

Chief among these: my editor, Jim Thomas, who helped me put the science into "science fiction" and tamed my prose into a manageable state; my agent, Erin Murphy, for tireless wisdom and necessary cheerleading; and Kimberly and Lauren, who provided critical plot brainstorming when this novel was still just an early blink in my story-brain.

To my wonderful writer friends who have helped along the way, with critiques, comments, advice, and encouragement: Kip Wilson, Natalie Lorenzi, Julie Phillipps, and the stellar Newton writers' group, as well as Kate Messner, Erin Dionne, Julie Berry, and Lisa Schulman.

For tireless help with my many scientific questions, especially assistance with the creation and dissection of the dread *Vermiletum:* Ed Loechler, Ben Clark, Sharon Nahill, and Livia Blackburne; and to Dr. Martin Weinberg for a most enlightening phone call about planetary rotation in a bisolar system.

To my local Starbucks, for being just the right kind of place for maximum writing efficiency, and to Arthur and Jen, Jim